He would overwhelm a woman

Flynn knew that loving him and being loved by him would be an all-consuming passion. There would be no room for reason; there would be no halfway measures. He would demand everything from the woman he wanted, heart and soul and body....

"You frighten me," she said, as the pulsing of her blood matched his.

"I'll never hurt you."

She looked at this man whom she had watched reign supreme with nothing but the power in his two fists and she believed him. "I trust you," she said softly, "and that frightens me even more."

Later, many people would say they were there when it happened. They would say it was as obvious as lightning across a summer sky and twice as electrifying. But, in truth, it was a small moment—a brief flicker of acknowledgment, of *destiny*, that left both Flynn and Jack shaken to their cores.

ABOUT THE AUTHOR

Barbara Bretton's published works range from stories in KATY KEENE comic books—written when she was ten years old—to articles in the *New York Times*, to contemporary and historical romances. Barbara, her husband, Roy, and their two parrots, Walter and Groucho, live in New Jersey. In *All We Know of Heaven*, she reprises some characters of the PAX organization from her previous books #274 *A Fine Madness*, #251 *Honeymoon Hotel* and #193 *Playing for Time*.

Books by Barbara Bretton

HARLEQUIN AMERICAN ROMANCE

138–THE EDGE OF FOREVER
161–PROMISES IN THE NIGHT
175–SHOOTING STAR
193–PLAYING FOR TIME
211–SECOND HARMONY
230–NOBODY'S BABY
251–HONEYMOON HOTEL
274–A FINE MADNESS
305–MOTHER KNOWS BEST
322–MRS. SCROOGE

HARLEQUIN INTRIGUE

18–STARFIRE

BARBARA BRETTON

ALL WE KNOW OF HEAVEN

Harlequin Books

TORONTO • NEW YORK • LONDON
AMSTERDAM • PARIS • SYDNEY • HAMBURG
STOCKHOLM • ATHENS • TOKYO • MILAN

"Parting is all we know of heaven
And all we need of hell."

—Emily Dickinson,
"My life closed twice before its close"

For Dallas,
who understands all about second chances

Published August 1990

ISBN 0-373-16355-X

PART I

Chapter One

Joe Cabrello loved weddings. Not only did he get time-and-a-half, he got to be around people who weren't rushing to make a plane or racing to some big business deal.

No hassles. No arguments. Just a lot of happy, smiling people in their fancy wedding finery, looking to have the time of their lives. He glanced in the rearview mirror of the sleek white Rolls-Royce he was driving that Sunday in July. It wasn't often you saw four young people as flat-out gorgeous as the quartet in the rear of the limo. The best man and maid of honor looked as if they were straight out of central casting while the bride and groom—Joe shook his head in bemusement. Hell, they almost made him start believing in happily-ever-after the way he used to when he was a kid.

Mary Scott had been out of the headlines for a long time now. Last time he'd seen her was on "Eyewitness News" when they'd covered her graduation from that fancy high school in Connecticut. She'd looked all freckle-faced and cute, nothing like the stunner sitting in the back of the Rolls. Joe wouldn't even have recognized her if he hadn't happened to overhear her new husband call her by her full name. Just goes to show what a few years of growing up could do.

Yeah, Joe Cabrello liked weddings, all right. He patted the bottle on the seat next to him. Someone always saw fit to give the limo driver a bottle of something extra-special so the wait for picture-taking up at the Cloisters wasn't so bad.

Today was no exception. Only this time the bearer of good tidings was another driver up there on the orange blossom special, same as Joe. Johnny Walker Black... He'd managed to polish off half a bottle while he waited. Time really flew when you got the right fuel in your engine. He stopped for a light and took another look in the rearview mirror at the little girl America had watched grow up before their eyes.

Presidents' daughters really knew how to treat their employees, he thought. Mary Scott had made certain he'd been paid right up front—and double time for Sunday, too. He'd expected a snooty, nose-up-in-the-air type, but she was real regular, not at all like those society dames he sometimes schlepped out to the Hamptons for meetings of their garden clubs.

He felt like he knew her. Twice he came close to asking about the pony she used to play with on the south lawn of the White House but managed to catch himself. None of your business, Cabrello. Kid had a right to a life of her own. She sure as shooting didn't need him sticking his two cents in, even if she did seem like one of the family.

Joe looked at the clock in the dashboard. The reception was due to start at the Plaza in ten minutes and he was still up in the Bronx. His own damn fault. He'd lost track of time back at the Cloisters, chewing the fat with Mr. Johnny Walker Black and not paying attention to business. Good thing his newfound pal had told him about a shortcut that would get him to midtown in a flash. "No lights, no cops, no traffic," the dark-haired guy had said, swigging down some rum when no one was looking. "Only way to go."

Can't disappoint Mary Flynn Scott, Joe thought and stomped on the accelerator.

IN THE BACK of the Rolls-Royce, Mary Flynn Scott Pennington looked at her brand-new husband and wished that she could stop time, for surely this was the most wonderful moment of her life.

Those ancient and beautiful words spoken in front of Father DeAngelis just an hour before lingered inside her head. Simple, powerful phrases of love and commitment that had changed her life forever. The sparkling circle of diamonds on the ring finger of her left hand was visible proof of the eternal promise they had made.

"Any regrets?" asked Billy Pennington, his dark eyes warm and tender.

"Only that we waited so long."

"You're only nineteen, Mary," he said, stroking her cheek with his index finger. "As it is, I'm robbing the cradle." Billy was the twenty-six-year-old son of the late Secretary of State. He was wealthy, accomplished and exceptionally handsome, one of the best and the brightest this nation had to offer. The world was spread out before him like a carpet of diamonds; political gossip had it that he was a natural to run for the House next year. Whispers of a Scott-Pennington dynasty were heard from Washington, D.C., to New York and back again.

But to Mary, he was simply the man she loved. Billy had pushed her on the swings, repaired her broken doll carriage, teased her about her braces, and given her her very first kiss. Through every crisis and triumph of her young life, it had been Billy who stood beside her. It seemed to Mary she had known him from the cradle and loved him just as long.

Across from them, Sara and David, their maid of honor and best man, laughed uproariously at something the driver had said and then turned the radio up.

Billy leaned toward Mary. His lips brushed against the curve of her ear, and a flood of longing swept over her, so fierce and sudden that for a moment she could not breathe.

"Tonight," he said in a voice meant for her alone. "Tonight you'll finally be mine."

A delicious shiver of anticipation rippled up Mary's spine. Tonight she would become both woman and wife in every way. Who would have believed it? There it was, the midpoint of 1980, and the virginal Mary Scott trembled at the thought of her wedding night.

Foolish little Mary, her friends had teased her, waiting for her wedding night before she took the plunge. "It's a new world, Mare," they said as they flitted from Studio 54 to Xenon—to hell and back again. "What are you waiting for?

Enjoy yourself.

Live dangerously."

This was the age of free sex, of experimentation, of taking what you wanted, damn the consequences.

But not for Mary. She was the daughter of one of the most beloved presidents the United States had known. A country had watched her grow up on the screens of their color televisions. She believed in the old values of love and commitment, of family and country, of honor and trust.

When her father died in office just after her fourteenth birthday, a country had turned to her for guidance during the terrible days before his funeral, much as the nation had turned to John F. Kennedy's widow that black November in 1963.

Frederick Scott had been a robust man, one who radiated good health. Photographers had a field day, snapping candid shots of the athletic young president running marathons, pumping iron, swimming speed laps in the White House pool.

His death at Camp David one lovely spring weekend shocked the nation and the world. An aneurysm, the experts had declared. A tiny rupture in a blood vessel in the brain, as swift and silent as the night wind, had taken his life and left his daughter alone.

But Mary had done her father proud. She held her head high, and although her heart ached for the only parent she'd ever known, she had pulled the grieving nation together with her fragile beauty and steely strength.

And now it was her turn.

Tonight she would give herself to her husband in soul and in body. All that she had, all that she would ever be, belonged to the man she loved. He took her hand in his, tracing slow sensuous circles on the fleshy base of her thumb, and she caught fire. Beyond the window of the air-conditioned Rolls, the city street shimmered with heat that found its match deep in Mary's belly and between her thighs. Her breasts ached with need. A vivid image of Billy's mouth tugging at her nipple made her cheeks flame as the low rumble of his chuckle tickled her ear.

"Not much longer, Mrs. Pennington," said her husband. "Just a few more hours..."

JACK FLANAGAN leaned against the window of a deli on Third Avenue. His heart pounded violently in his ears. His breathing came fast and shallow. Bile burned his throat and filled his mouth with fear.

Do it, man, the voice inside his head urged. *Just go in there and do it!*

He wasn't blind. He knew the way life really was. He'd grown up watching the dark-eyed men with sleek black Caddy Eldorados and shiny sharkskin suits, and he knew that money was the answer. *It takes money to get money...money talks...who says money can't buy happiness?*

Money changed everything. Money could turn a beggar into a king.

The opportunities were everywhere: an unminded cash register; a wallet peeking from a back pocket; pocketbooks dangling over old ladies' shoulders.

What in hell was he waiting for? Nothing was going to change. That stinking apartment in Brooklyn wasn't going to turn into a penthouse. His brothers and sisters weren't going to suddenly come back to Brooklyn and whisk Ma and Katherine out of that rat-infested hole in the wall. Ma would get older and weaker, and he knew in his gut there was no miracle hiding around the corner for Katherine; she would never leave, never marry, never venture beyond the front door of their apartment.

It was up to him. All of it. The need and the fear and the endless nights of wanting something more, of looking for a way out, a chance to—

To what? He'd been down so long he didn't even remember how to dream.

He reached under his T-shirt and felt the handgun tucked into the waistband of his jeans. He'd found it hidden under a mattress in his brother's apartment in Queens. It was Jack's now. It would make everything possible.

Scanning the street, he turned, then entered the deli.

"TWO KIDS," SAID BILLY, as the Rolls-Royce exited the highway and eased into the Manhattan traffic. "One boy. One girl. He'll have my looks and Mary's brains. She'll be exactly like her mother."

The future shimmered before Mary, seductive and bright. She wanted to race headlong and embrace it. Savor all of the wonderful dreams that were finally— amazingly!—coming true.

"Four children," she said, certain as only a nineteen-year-old girl can be. "Two boys and two girls. All geniuses." They were as real to her as this man she loved, these friends she cherished. Children of her heart and imagination, soon to be real.

"Looks like you have your work cut out for you, pal," said David, their best man. "This girl means business."

"Woman," corrected Sara, glaring at her fiancé. "This is 1980. We're not girls anymore."

Mary's quick smile was for her husband's eyes alone. *Soon*, her look said. Soon he would take her in his arms and make her the woman she longed to be for him. Her heart ached with love and desire. "I wish we could skip the dinner." It was only to be an intimate dinner, with their best friends Sara and David. Surely, they would understand. Her lips brushed his ear and she laughed softly at the look of desire in his eyes.

"I wish..." He told her exactly what he wished for. His breath was warm; his words were flame.

Mary reddened and looked out the window, pressing her hot cheek against the cool glass. Their wedding had been spur of the moment, although the feelings between them had existed for a very long time. Billy's family was gone, and Mary had no one except for her Uncle Hugh, who was busy with important international matters in Geneva. Uncle Hugh had wanted her to wait, to have the lavish traditional ceremony befitting the daughter of a former president, but Mary's heart had said otherwise. Mary and Billy took it as a sign of the rightness of things that they were able to put their wedding supper together on such short notice—and without utilizing the illustrious Scott or Pennington names. "I think you're crazy," Sara had said as she phoned for reservations. "The name Spencer doesn't pull much weight in this town, but I'm glad to help."

They wanted no publicity, no newshounds sniffing at their heels. Her uncle would understand. After all, he had cared for her selflessly from the moment her father died; she knew he only wanted the best for her, and Billy Pennington was certainly that.

At that moment she wasn't a president's daughter; she was a woman in love, and women in love didn't wait.

Besides, what was the point to waiting? They wanted to spend their lives together. Why waste one instant of life, one moment of happiness?

The Rolls slowed to a stop at a traffic light, and a girl in tan shorts and a navy polo shirt peered curiously at the white limousine. Mary wanted to fling open the door and shout her happiness at the pedestrians on the street corner. She wanted to toast the world with champagne and toss red roses to the children playing in the spray from the fire hydrant.

She'd waited all her life for this moment, and now, more than anything, she wanted to begin her life with Billy.

"I'M NOT GIVIN' YOU NOTHIN'." The teenaged clerk's Adam's apple bobbed with each word. "I'm callin' the cops."

Jack's hand trembled violently. Sweat made it hard to grip the gun, and he prayed his size would intimidate the kid. "Open that register now," he roared. "You've got five seconds or I'll..." His words trailed off. He wondered if the kid knew he was bluffing, that there was nothing in that gun but frustration and rage.

The clerk's eyes widened. His watery gaze darted from the gun to Jack then back again. Jack watched as the kid pushed a button and the cash register drawer flew open, catching him in the stomach. "Here." He pushed a handful of bills toward Jack. "That's all I got."

Jack stared at the money. Three twenty-dollar bills, a dozen or so tens and some fives. A lousy two hundred if he was lucky. "You're holding out on me."

The kid raised his hands, palms outward. He blinked once, twice, a dozen times in quick succession. "Swear to God I'm not."

What are you going to do, big shot? Make the kid cry? He jammed the bills into his pocket and backed toward the door. "Keep your hands off the alarm."

"We don't have an alarm."

"Make noise and I'll come back and finish the job."

"I won't do nothin'. Honest."

Of course he wouldn't. He was a good kid. Sixteen, maybe seventeen. Probably the kind of kid Jack would've been if life had played him a different hand. He pushed through the door and hit the street. A knot of people waited at the corner for the light to change. Jack stood for a moment behind a blonde who smelled of Shalimar but the panic rose up into his throat, choking him.

He darted into the traffic, sidestepping a kamikaze cab driver and skimming the bumper of a red Mercedes with DPL plates. The money scratched against his skin with every step. The gun pressed against his rib cage. He beat the traffic light at the next corner then jaywalked the one after that, aware of the curious glances tossed his way.

The air was thick and hot. Humidity lay across his shoulders like a wet wool blanket. *Don't think about it.* He jostled a man with a cane as he hurried past. *You did what you had to do.*

From somewhere behind him came the sharp cry of a police car. He started to run, trying to force air into his burning lungs, keeping pace with the thudding beat of his heart. Forty-second and Second Avenue...Fiftieth Street...the corner of Park and Fifty-third...the girls in their summer dresses...men with briefcases filled with important papers...the money in his pocket burned hotter than the sidewalk beneath his feet....

The fountain at the Plaza Hotel at 59th and Fifth shimmered in the gathering dusk, and he stopped, mesmerized, as a big white Rolls-Royce eased into the intersection. The fancy hood ornament glittered, taunting him with all the things he would never have, all the things he would never be. Somebody had dropped a bundle on that car. Probably more money than Jack would earn in his entire life. The two hundred dollars burning a hole through his back pocket was pocket change to the guy who—

And then he saw her, so quick a glimpse of heaven that for a moment he thought he'd died and an angel had come to fetch his soul. Her delicate, heart-shaped face was framed in white lace, and he imagined the scent of violets in the air around him. A bride, he thought, as envy washed over him. Another man's wife.

The beautiful bride was saying something, smiling joyously, when she turned toward him, and he knew she was everything on earth he wanted and would never have. Her eyes were large and dark, and the look she gave him was one of such pure happiness that he knew no one would ever look at him that way again.

He wanted to get closer to her. The Rolls was stopped in the intersection, waiting to turn. He stepped off the curb then darted toward the car when he heard a pop-like gunshot. Then the roar of an engine sounded from his right, and he leaped back onto the curb as an out-of-control yellow cab barreled into the intersection and headed straight for the Rolls.

Chapter Two

The yellow cab slammed into the white Rolls at full speed with a sickening shriek of tires. Cars squealed to a stop, skittering crazily across the intersection. Women screamed at the bone-crushing sound of metal against metal, and men swore into the hot summer air. The high distant wail of a cop's car echoed down the long city block, lights flashing against the gathering darkness.

A cry tore its way up from Jack's gut but was lost in the chaos. His mind was empty of everything but pure adrenaline-fueled rage.

"Forget it, pal!" A burly man in a stained T-shirt grabbed Jack around the waist and struggled to hold him back. "Ain't nobody left in there!"

Jack brushed the man off as if he were a speck of dust then darted into the street. She was alive. He knew she was alive. That beautiful bride with her entire perfect life still ahead of her was trapped inside the burning wreck of the limo, and Jack knew he was her last chance.

Waves of heat stopped him a few feet away from the twisted vehicles. He caught the stench of burning hair and blood, and his stomach lurched. "Give it up!" screamed a voice from behind him. "The gas tanks are gonna blow!"

Tongues of orange flame swept over what was left of the yellow cab, dancing closer and closer to the gas tank on the limo. The inside of the Rolls was dark. He squinted against the smoke and made out the outline of a man's body and the frothy whiteness of a wedding gown against the shattered interior. A bouquet of white roses and yellow freesia lay incongruously on the ground near his feet.

A wall of sound rose up from the flames, a violent hurricane-rush of noise that ignited something close to panic inside his belly. "They're all dead," shouted someone behind him. "You lookin' to kill yourself, man?"

He reached for the door. His flesh hissed as it touched the red-hot metal. *Don't start playing Boy Scout now,* his brain cried. In his whole stinking life he'd never done one brave or generous thing. If he had half a brain, he'd turn around now and disappear back into the night before the whole street went up like a thousand rockets on the Fourth of July.

And then he saw it, a movement so slight he thought he'd imagined it. A tiny rustle of white satin and lace, a low keening wail that tore his heart in two and breathed life into the emptiness that had been his soul for longer than he could remember.

His flesh sizzled against hot steel. His eyes watered from the smoke. The muscles of his back and forearms contorted with pain as he struggled to open the bashed-in door. He felt none of it. He heard only the rapid flutter of her breathing, saw only the blood staining her pale skin and the bruises obscuring her beauty, felt only the ancient, powerful desire to hold Death off with both hands.

And Death was everywhere in that wrecked limousine. Jack willed himself to see none of it, to let none of it matter. There was only the girl who lay crumpled at his feet in a cloud of sorrowful lace.

Her eyes—as blue as he'd known they would be—fluttered open, and she struggled to focus in on him. "Billy?" Her voice was as sweet as birdsong, as soft as the wings of a butterfly. "Oh, Billy, is that you?"

"Yes, it's Billy." He'd gladly give up twenty years of his life to be the man she loved, if only for a moment. "I'm here. I'll take care of you."

He twisted his way closer to the girl. His lungs burned as he struggled for air in the heavy, acrid smoke that filled what was left of the Rolls.

"You got thirty seconds," a fire fighter screamed from behind. "That sucker's ready to blow."

Jack's heart hammered wildly as his adrenaline surged. He didn't give a damn if he got out of there alive. Everything he cared about, everything he could ever want, was right there within reach. All that mattered was that she lived.

SCREAMING...THE SOUND of screaming every-where...the smell of blood...the sharp sting of metal against her flesh...death hovering overhead... unmistakable...inevitable.

It was hard to concentrate. Mary struggled to bring her thoughts together. The pathway was up ahead. She could just make out the ribbon of road in the darkness. Bright lights pierced her closed lids and she turned her head away. How could she think with all these distractions? What was it she was supposed to do?

She shifted slightly, her hip bumping up against a piece of metal. How strange. Why was she so uncomfortable? Nothing made sense. Billy. She would ask Billy. Billy could answer all of her questions.

But Billy wasn't there. Not really. She knew that. Billy was calling for her. He waited up at the end of that curving road. *I'm trying, Billy. I'm trying but I can't seem to reach you.* She walked and walked and never left this cold and wet place, the shattered back seat of the wedding car. Sara and David were there with Billy, laughing and waving toward her. *I want to be with you. Help me! Meet me halfway....*

Prayers from her childhood filled her heart and mind. *Now*, she prayed to the God she'd once trusted. *Take me with them...don't ask me to go on with no one...with nothing...*

A strong pair of arms lifted her up from the cold, encircling her, cradling her against a fiery warmth. Yes, this was it. This was her time, just as she'd thought. Her father was up ahead, too, calling her name. Her tears burned across her cheeks, searing her skin. *Everyone...everything that matters. Can't you do something, Daddy? Can't you make this all go away?*

Any second she'd be with her husband and father, with the mother whose memory had grown painfully dim over the years.

"I'll take care of you," a deep voice said. A man's voice. Strong and comforting. "Don't worry."

I believe you, she thought. *I'm almost home.*

SHE WAS LIGHT as the summer air in his arms. Jack wished he could hold her forever. But forever was coming at him fast, and he was running out of time. A wall of fire moved toward him, and he pressed her delicate face against his shoulder, coughing as the hot smoky air burned his throat and robbed his lungs of oxygen. Time kaleidoscoped around him; distance snake-danced crazily. He was tired and disoriented, and only the scream of a fire engine served to lead him back to the light.

"Get the girl!" It seemed to Jack that a hundred ambulance technicians rushed in at him and he backed away, gasping for air.

"Keep away!" he screamed, cradling the bride closer to his chest as, behind them, the limo exploded with a mighty roar. "She's all right. I've got her."

"She's bleeding, man." A bearded ambulance technician stepped closer to Jack. His voice was low, calm. "Let us do our thing."

Her blood was on him. Her breathing was shallow, labored. She was dying with each second that passed. "I'm not leaving her," he said as he let the medics take the bride from the protection of his arms. "I'm going with her."

"The hell you are." A young cop elbowed his way between Jack and the girl. "You're coming with me. We need a statement and—"

Jack spun around toward the cop, fists clenched, but the bearded ambulance technician stepped in. "Get your statement at the hospital," he suggested while the medics struggled frantically over the young bride. "This guy's comin' with us."

The cop lit into the technician but none of it penetrated. Jack's breath rose and fell with the girl's; his heartbeat slowed, weakened.

"Look at this!" roared the technician, spinning Jack around to face the young cop. "The man's got second-degree burns. He needs help."

"I need a statement," said the cop.

The technician spat out a curse and jerked his head toward the blazing vehicles in the intersection. "Worry about that, why don't you?"

All Jack remembered later about the ride to the hospital was the smell of fear. He shivered uncontrollably in the air-conditioned ambulance as they hooked up an IV to her slender arm.

"BP, 100 over 65," barked an attendant. "Pulse 108...thready..."

"Move it!" screamed an intern with glasses and an overbite. "We're losing her."

Jack dragged his hands through his hair, feeling that age-old sense of rage settle over him, smothering hope. "Do something," he pleaded. "Don't let her die!"

The intern eyed him suspiciously. "You know her?"

"I—"

"Billy." The bride's whisper pierced the ambulance. "Billy, are you—"

Jack was at her side with her next breath, holding her hand between his. "I'm here." His words were for her alone. Nothing in that ambulance held any reality for him except this girl. "I'll always be here."

"...hurt..." She paused, moistening her cracked lips with the tip of her tongue. "...so thirsty..."

He looked up and an attendant nodded. He grabbed a cup of water from the intern and gently wet her mouth with a sliver of ice. A faint smile crossed her features. *She doesn't know,* he thought. *She doesn't know anything.* He wished there were some way to shield her from the truth forever, to take her and run to a place were none of this could ever hurt her again.

But, of course, he couldn't.

This was New York City, a place where dreams didn't last the night. A place where money talked and little else mattered. A place where bums from Brooklyn and girls like the beautiful bride didn't have a chance in hell.

"Billy?" That voice again, that angel-wing voice. He bent down and placed his ear against her lips. "I love you, Billy."

"I know," he said, tears falling against her cheek. "I won't let you go."

A TEAM OF SURGEONS WAITED at the hospital. An operating room was ready, and the bride was whisked from Jack's sight seconds after they blasted through the swinging doors of the Emergency Room. The young cop and an even younger reporter collared Jack before he had a chance to ask where in hell he was.

"Name?" asked the cop, pencil poised over his clipboard.

"Flanagan." He hesitated, suddenly aware of the money jammed into the waistband of his jeans. "Uh... Billy Flanagan."

"Address?"

He stumbled over the street number. He'd been raised in a neighborhood where the police were the enemy and anonymity was your best defense.

"What were you doing at the scene?"

Blood pounded in his ears. For one crazy moment he wanted to bolt and run; only the thought of the girl kept him rooted to the spot.

"I was heading toward the Park."

The cop nodded. His pencil made scratching sounds against the paper. Jack reached behind him to feel for the money but yelped as his hand encountered raw flesh.

"You need a doctor, pal," said the reporter, peering at Jack through bright blue contacts. "You're one hell of a mess."

Jack glanced at the guy but said nothing. Last thing he needed was to strip down for some medic and be forced to explain the money drifting to the floor like confetti.

The cop inclined his head in the general direction of the OR. "Gimme her name."

"I don't know it."

The cop's eyebrows lifted. "Whaddaya mean, you don't know her name?"

"Just what I said." *Stay cool, Flanagan. You're asking for trouble.* "I've never seen her before."

"Risked your life to save a stranger?"

Jack shrugged.

"Jane Doe," said the cop, pencil skating across the page. "Just what we need."

"If she lives, you're a hero," said the reporter, yanking a small camera from his jacket pocket. "Front page material."

Jack snapped out of his haze long enough to cover the lens with his hand. "No."

"Come on," urged the reporter. "Just one. Something to show the guys in the neighborhood."

He tightened his grip on the lens, and the reporter flushed an angry red. "Keep me out of it."

The reporter tried to stare him down, but Jack was bigger and stronger. The reporter straightened his lapels and jammed his camera back into his pocket. "I'm not gonna waste good copy on this."

The cop waited until the reporter drifted off in search of hotter news. "You sure you don't know her?"

"Positive," said Jack.

"No ID on her," the cop mumbled, shaking his head. "Damn cars were burned to cinders. No ID left on anybody."

"She'll tell you," offered Jack. Once she was out of surgery and awake, she'd tell them who she was and where she lived, and her world would draw her back inside.

"Not if she dies, she won't." The cop jammed the pencil back into his pocket. "You don't look so good," he told Jack. "Better see a doctor yourself."

Jack reluctantly submitted to an exam by a burn specialist who shrugged and muttered, "I've seen worse," then sauntered off in search of more expensive prey. No one even questioned the two hundred dollars stuffed into his pocket.

They covered his back with a salve and a light layer of bandages. He supposed there was pain; every now and again a stab of fierce heat registered itself in his brain, but it didn't matter. All he could think about were the cop's offhanded words: *Not if she dies, she won't... not if she dies, she won't... not if she dies...*

The nurses gave him wide berth as he paced the lobby of the ER. One, a brunette with kind eyes, offered him a glass of iced tea, but he shook his head.

"Any word?" He felt huge and clumsy, like some wild beast trapped in a cell.

The nurse looked away. "The moment we hear something..." Her words trailed off. It didn't take a genius to see that Jack was the only one who held out any hope.

"Go home, young man," said the supervisor, a tiny gray-haired woman. "You need rest."

"Forget it."

"I could have you escorted home."

He laughed out loud. She treated him as if he was five years old. "Yeah? And who would escort the escort back?"

"Rough neighborhood?" she asked, a smile lighting her lined face.

"The roughest. The outskirts of Bed-Stuy."

"I'm from Hell's Kitchen myself," she said, winking. "We go to Brooklyn when we need a vacation."

He touched her arm. "I gotta know about the girl. Will she... I mean do you think she'll—"

"I can't answer that, son. You can pray."

Pray? Jack wouldn't know where to begin. His mother said her endless rosaries night after night, and it brought her nothing but heartache. It had been years since Jack had stepped foot inside a church. Not since his old man's funeral. All his tears and prayers hadn't been enough to bring his father back to life.

No reason to think he'd have better luck this time.

AGAIN IT WAS the bright light that drew her forward.

Mary moaned and turned her head away. She wanted to sleep. More than anything, she wanted to sink back into the welcoming darkness and sleep. Why couldn't they understand?

"Come on, honey." A woman's voice urged her toward that light. "Open your eyes."

She would do anything if they would just leave her alone. She opened her eyes, but nothing happened. Somehow her eyelids weren't receiving the message from her brain. What was wrong? Why was it so hard to perform such a simple task?

"That's it," said the woman with the soft voice. "A little more... good... good."

The room was hazy, like a watercolor painting viewed through gauze. She blinked once, then twice, struggling to bring her surroundings into focus.

"Can you see me?" A shadowy figure bent over Mary, blocking out the shocking glare.

"Ye-es." Her throat was raw, as if someone had sandpapered the length of it when Mary wasn't looking. She coughed to clear her throat but the pain was daunting.

"Don't worry," said the woman, middle-aged and soothingly plump. "You were entubated. That pinch you're feeling is normal."

The woman moved to the right and once again Mary was bathed in glare from a huge round fluorescent fixture on the ceiling.

"Do you know where you are?" The woman was wearing a shirt of dusty green cotton.

"I don't know... a hospital?" That would explain the bone-deep pain that seemed to be floating just out of reach, the sense of exhaustion so overpowering she longed to give way to it.

"Yes, dear." The woman brushed a lock of hair off Mary's forehead. How easy it would be to close her eyes again and imagine this was her mother, that she was a little girl once more, all safe and protected and happy in the circle of her family's love.

The woman shook her gently and Mary's eyes fluttered open again. "Do you know what year it is, dear?"

"1980," said Mary.

"Who is president?"

"Jimmy Carter." Mary giggled as the room spun slowly around. What silly questions.

"And your name?"

Now there you've got me.

"Honey, do you know your name?"

Daddy. Elvis. Mickey Mouse. "Billy. Yes." She nodded. "Billy."

"Rest now, honey," said the nurse. "We'll take you to your room in a few minutes."

JACK WAS SPRAWLED on his stomach across a strip of plastic chairs in the ER waiting room. His feet dangled off one end, his head drooped over the other. The burns on his back were a thousand individual trips to hell, and he was so tired he was hallucinating. Twice they'd tried to get him to go home and twice he'd told them exactly what they could do with their well-meaning advice. He wasn't going any place until he found out what had happened to her.

On the television set suspended from the ceiling, Lucy Ricardo begged and pleaded, but Ricky still wouldn't let her be in the show. Her high-pitched wail blended in with the ambulance siren in the parking lot. He wanted to put his fist through the screen and shut that noise up forever. He closed his eyes more tightly, forcing himself to lie still. To wait.

"Son?"

He shot to his feet, nearly toppling the gray-haired nurse from Hell's Kitchen. "She's dead." The words had a life of their own.

"She's not dead." Her smile was as real as the relief that grabbed him by the throat. "She's in recovery."

"I want to see her."

The head nurse narrowed her eyes. "You related?"

Jack could lie with the best of them but, oddly, he found it tough to lie to her. "No. I—"

She patted his forearm. "Can I convince you to go home and get some sleep? She'll be here when you wake up in the morning."

"I'm staying here."

"That's what I thought you'd say."

"I just wanna see that she's okay."

"An hour," said the head nurse, "maybe two."

"I'll be here."

He dozed fitfully. His dreams were a bizarre mix of the kid in the deli, his mother's face floating over the top of the church he hadn't been to in years, and the girl in the white limo. When he saw her safe in her pristine hospital bed, he'd feel differently. No one got under his skin; no one ever had. Not even his own family made him feel this exposed. He hated the aching, vulnerable emotions that fragile girl had brought to life inside his heart from his first glimpse of her through the tinted window of the Rolls. He would make sure that she was okay, and then he would walk out of that hospital and forget this whole thing ever happened.

Just before midnight shift change, the head nurse shook him gently awake and led him down the darkened hallway toward the girl's room. He was half-asleep, groggy from exhaustion and pain, and he found it hard to keep up with the older woman's pace.

The nurse skidded to a stop before a door marked "Jane Doe—No Smoking." The gray-haired woman caught the look of confusion on his face. "Amnesia," she said, her tone unconcerned. "Usually temporary. Happens often after head injuries."

He nodded as if he knew what she was talking about. Head injuries . . . that beautiful face. His heart thudded the way it had when he pulled the girl from the burning limo.

"What are you waiting for?" asked the nurse with a laugh. "Go on in." She placed her hands against the small of his back, and before he knew what hit him, he was inside the room, alone with the girl.

"Hello." That angel-wing voice. Soft and gently husky. Would he ever forget the sound? "Sorry I can't shake hands."

He stepped closer and quickly took in the casts on one arm and leg, the heavy swath of bandages across her forehead and on her right shoulder, the oxygen tank ready for emergencies. Her delicately beautiful face was obscured by the hideous bruises and ugly swelling. Only her eyes—those innocent eyes—were as he remembered. He saw it all and he saw none of it because she smiled at him—for *him* and nobody else—and in that instant he was well and truly lost.

Chapter Three

The man filled the door to Mary's hospital room, his broad shoulders grazing the jamb, dark eyes wary and uncertain as he watched her.

"I—uh, I—" He stumbled over his words, his tanned face growing red with embarrassment. "Hi."

She tried to smile but even that simple movement left pain in its wake. "Please sit," she managed, glancing toward the hard backed chair to the right of the oxygen tank.

He folded his long limbs into the tiny chair. He was the largest man Mary had seen in her entire life. Easily five inches over the six-foot mark, with hands that looked as if they were made to hold a basketball the way another man held an apple. She had the feeling that in her real life—whatever it might be—this man would have frightened her.

There was an anger about him, a high-voltage tension that sizzled in the darkened hospital room.

"How you feeling?" His voice was gruff and deep, yet not without a touch of tenderness.

"Tired." She moistened her lips, struggling to fight off the effects of the painkiller dripping slowly into her veins through the IV. "They—they say you helped me."

He shrugged and looked away. "No big deal."

She wanted to tell him it was a big deal, that she didn't know what had happened to her, that it seemed as if her whole life had disappeared in the time it took to blink her eyes, that the only real thing in the universe at that moment was the look in his dark blue eyes as she faded slowly down the rabbit hole with Alice once again....

JACK STARED AS SHE DRIFTED back into unconsciousness. He'd never seen a woman so terrifyingly fragile. Her light blond hair was matted and drawn back from her fine-boned face into a ponytail. A portion over her left temple had been shaved, and an ugly slash, bisected by stitches, drew his eye. She was so slender that she barely made a bump under the taut white sheets. The casts on her right arm and right leg overpowered her.

Even now, without the limousine and the beautiful wedding dress and the trappings of wealth surrounding her, he knew she was unlike anyone he'd ever known. There was a purity to her, an innocence he'd only seen on movie screens. You didn't see girls like that in Brooklyn. In his world, dark streets and simmering angers took care of innocence in short order. His sisters had been streetwise before they were old enough to date. It didn't take a genius to see this beautiful girl had been protected all of her young life. Hell, despite her pain, she'd been lady enough to smile and offer him a seat as if they were in the drawing room of some ritzy home on Park Avenue.

The last person to offer him a seat had been a cop at the Twelfth Precinct the day Jack stole a hubcap from a mafioso's black Caddy.

He sat there quietly, watching the gentle rise and fall of her chest. Her left hand was curled across her stomach. Pale blue veins showed clearly against the milky white of her skin. He could live to be one hundred and still never get this close to heaven again.

The head nurse appeared at his side. "She needs her sleep," the nurse said, motioning toward the girl. She laid a hand on Jack's shoulder. "So do you."

"I'm not going." He looked up into the woman's eyes. "Not until I have to."

"I could make you, you know." He knew that tone of voice: Sister Mary Immaculata had used it on him in first grade.

"You won't."

"I should." The nurse's sigh drifted over his head. "But you're right. I won't."

He settled down to watch the sleeping girl.

SHE WAS ALIVE. Mary wasn't entirely certain she was happy about that fact. Her body was a network of disparate aches and sharp pains that vied for her attention.

"Morning, sleepyhead."

Even her eyelids hurt. Opening them to the morning sunshine was an exercise in agony. She saw two doors, two windows, two unbelievably tall men sitting in two small chairs next to her bed. The man who had rescued her? She struggled to bring the images into focus.

"I didn't imagine you."

"No." His face was impassive; only his eyes gave him away. They were sad eyes, the tender expression in them at odds with his macho stance.

So you aren't as tough as you look, are you? It was obvious he was used to intimidating people with the sheer force of his size. Sitting there in a tiny chair like an ordinary person must be hard for him. He wore his emotions uneasily, as if they were a coat that was two sizes too small, and Mary sensed he had little experience in dealing with subtleties like compassion and tenderness.

"You're smiling." He sounded surprised.

"I must be delirious," she said, her voice soft and husky. How foolish her thought would appear to him. How could she pretend to know what was inside his heart and soul when she couldn't even remember her own name?

"Do you hurt much?"

"Yes, but it almost feels like it's someone else's body." Which in a way it was—at least until her memory returned.

His smile was off-center and dazzling but quicksilver fast. "Felt that way the time I broke my leg." He made it sound like an everyday occurrence. "I knew it hurt like hell but I floated over it."

She motioned for him to pull his chair closer. The casts on her arm and leg made her feel helpless. "How did this happen? Was I mugged?"

That steady gaze of his darted toward the window then back again. "Car crash."

The blip of her heartbeat on the monitor increased. "Wh-where?"

"Hey, look—" He touched her arm, his skin hot and alive against her cold body. She wished she could disappear into his arms and make the unknown vanish in the blink of an eye. "I don't know what I'm supposed to say to you. I don't know what they've told you."

"They've told me nothing," she said vehemently. "No one looks at me, no one talks to me. I don't even know what city I'm in or who I am or—" Dear God, the tears were quick and fierce, coursing down her cheeks despite her struggle to regain control.

"New York." He touched her cheek with the back of his huge hand. "The east side. The accident happened near the park."

"I want to remember," she said, closing her eyes and praying for her memory to return. "I want to know..."

"You were with some people." He stumbled over his words, as if he wanted to rid himself of their meaning. "They—you're the only one who..." His voice drifted off into the air.

"I knew it," she whispered. That heavy ache inside her chest wasn't the result of broken ribs; it was the pain of a broken heart. He told her of the fire, of the totalled car, and she could feel the flames and hear the scream of metal against metal, but she couldn't place herself in the middle of the agony. Everything he told her was true—she could feel the truth of his words inside her soul—but she wasn't ready for it. Not now. Possibly not ever.

All she wanted for the moment was to lie there and listen to his deep voice, bask in his warmth, pretend that when it all came back to her she would be strong enough to bear the truth.

JACK SAT WITH THE GIRL all day, leaving the room only when the doctors and technicians came by to poke and prod and make pronouncements you'd need a master's degree to understand. "Selective amnesia," a white-coated doctor said. "The mind shuts down so the body can heal. See it all the time." Her condition was upgraded and Jack overheard talk of taking her off the monitor within the next forty-eight hours.

"That's one lucky girl," the head nurse told him in the hallway the second night as the girl slept. "She should be dead."

"It wasn't her time." He didn't go for talk like this. It didn't come easy for him to talk about what was or what might have been. All he understood was the here and now.

"Because of you, boy." The nurse reached up and touched his chin, forcing him to meet her curious gaze. "But you do know it's not going to last, don't you? If it wasn't the holiday weekend, they'd probably have ID'd the car by now."

Don't look at me like that. Don't go trying to figure out what's in my head. "Yeah," he mumbled, moving just beyond her reach.

That little gray-haired nurse was more than a match for him. "Listen to me. They're looking for her people. You'll be pushed aside before you know what hit you."

"Won't be the first time."

"Think you're tough, don't you?"

He hated the way she looked at him, her eyes clouded with pity. "I found her. It's my responsibility to stay with her. Nothing more than that."

"And when her people come for her?"

He shrugged, pretending the nurse's words weren't aimed straight at his gut. "Then it's over. Big deal."

"Big deal," repeated the nurse, shaking her head. "A bigger deal than you know."

"You don't know what you're talking about, old lady," he exploded, unable to control the inward rush of emotion that forced the breath from his lungs. "I don't need nobody telling me how I feel. I do what I want." He didn't need lectures about love and honor and all the other hollow emotions and virtues people like her put so much stock in. "Keep your damned nose out of my business."

The small nurse packed a huge wallop. His cheek stung from the force of her hand. "Selfish bastard," she said, her voice calm and reasonable. "It's the girl I'm thinking about. Play one mind game on her, hotshot, and I'll have your butt tossed out on the street so fast your head will spin."

He could have decked her. She was old and small, and it wouldn't have taken much to grab her up and scare the living hell out of her. He wanted to—God, how much he wanted to. But there was still some small shred of civilized behavior left inside him that poverty and the city hadn't destroyed, and that small shred of civilized behavior held him back.

Besides, there was one other factor at play: the nurse was one hundred percent right. If he had his way, the beautiful bride in the hospital room would never regain her memory. She'd be his forever.

SHE SLEPT THROUGH THE NIGHT, leaving Jack alone and uncomfortable with his thoughts. He washed in the visitors' bathroom down the hall and was startled when the crumpled bills spilled from the pocket of his jeans and onto the tiled floor. He leaned against the sink, sweat breaking out behind his neck and running down his back.

Some kind of hero, he thought, staring down at the money. "You'll be headline news," that reporter had said the night of the crash. "If she lives, you'll be on the front page of every paper in town."

Yeah. Right. Criminal saves girl's life. What a heartwarming story. He'd been desperate when he knocked over the deli. He was still desperate. Nothing had changed. He'd had all those high and mighty ideas about getting money for Ma and Katherine, about trying to make it easier on them and put food on the table. None of it had even been close to the truth.

He did it because he wanted to. Because he needed the money. Because there wasn't any other way in the whole damned world for him to get ahead. Two hundred dollars wasn't a whole hell of a lot, but it was more than he'd ever had at one time in his life. He could pay part of the back rent or buy a big steak dinner or—

He bent down and scooped up the money. Before he had a chance to change his mind, he strode down the hallway toward the cashier's office.

"Can I help you?" The clerk with the thinning hair looked as if he had his hand poised over the police alarm.

Jack pushed the crumpled bills through the opening in the Plexiglas shield. "Jane Doe," he said. "Room 402. I wanna put this toward her tab."

The clerk's bushy red brows arched toward the ceiling. "You family?"

Jack bristled. "My money's not good enough?"

"Any money's good enough. I'm just asking." The clerk motioned vaguely toward a ledger propped against a battered copy of *Atlas Shrugged*. "For the record."

"Flanagan...John James Flanagan." *You crazy, Flanagan? You never give 'em your real name....*

The clerk smoothed the bills out with the heel of his manicured hand and cast a curious look at Jack. "They're running a trace on the dead female passenger and hope to get a make on the girl that way. If you know who our Jane Doe is and you're not telling, the guys in blue won't be too happy."

As if Jack cared what the NYPD thought. "If I knew who she was, I'd make sure she got to a better hospital than this."

The clerk's curiosity changed quickly to cold, hard anger. "You've got yourself one big chip on your shoulder, my friend. One day someone's going to come along and knock it off for you."

Jack's muscles tensed the way they did when he rode the subway late at night. All his life they'd been judging him, from Sister Mary Immaculata to the head nurse to this know-nothing clerk with the Coke-bottle glasses. Judging him and finding him wanting. *Cool it!* an inner voice warned. *Lose your temper now and you'll never see her again.*

"Credit her account, will you?" he asked, forcing himself to sound calm and rational while his demons fought to take control.

The clerk started to say something but thought better of it and shrugged. "It's your money."

Not exactly.

She was still asleep when he got back to her room. Painkiller dripped into her veins from the IV suspended from the metal trolley at the side of her bed and he smiled at the peaceful sound of her breathing. He'd never spent forty-eight hours in one room before in his life, much less forty-eight hours with a woman he wasn't sleeping with. It occurred to him he might as well be on another planet because it seemed as if his old life had disappeared the moment he saw her in that limousine.

Jack had no experience with gentleness. She was as helpless as an infant, dependent upon him to provide the bits and pieces that once were her life. He wanted to be honest with her. She deserved that much. There was steel beneath the satin of her skin. Laid up there in that hospital bed she managed to retain a sense of dignity that made him wonder which of them was really the stronger.

But how could he tell her she was a bride, that in the car crash she'd lost not only her friends, but her brand-new husband? The words wouldn't budge past the huge and painful lump in his throat. He'd heard them talking around the hospital. They'd identified one of the passengers and had a pretty good idea who the bride was. It didn't matter to him. If her people loved her, they'd be with her. The way he was.

What was it the doctor had said the other day—that sometimes the mind blocks out reality until the body is strong enough to deal with it. Maybe the girl wasn't ready to remember. Maybe she needed to heal her broken bones before she could manage to heal her broken heart.

She needed him. He was good for her—anybody could see the way she responded to him. He made her laugh with his stories. He stroked her hair when the pain and the fear made her cry. He could be anything she wanted him to be. With a woman like that beside him, he'd have a chance for the one thing he'd never dreamed possible for him.

He'd have a chance to be happy.

"PIZZA," SAID MARY on the morning of the fourth day. "The first thing I want when I'm released is pizza."

The man—*Jack*—grinned as he gulped down a glass of juice left behind for him by a nurse's aide. "Jell-O getting on your nerves?"

"I hate Jell-O," she said. "I bet I've always hated it." She lifted a spoonful of the jiggly, emerald-green stuff and wrinkled her nose. "Why on earth would anyone eat food that quivers?"

"Eat it. You're too skinny."

"I'm slender." She glanced down at her skinny form under the sheets. "There's a difference."

He leaned forward and speared a piece of scrambled egg with a fork. "If you hate Jell-O, then eat this."

She laughed. "I'm not a baby, Jack. I can feed myself."

"Not with that IV in your arm."

The scrambled egg was cold and rubbery, but she forced it down anyway. She wanted to make his serious face light up with a smile. "How old do you think I am?"

The question seemed to unnerve him. A patch of red appeared on his cheekbones, but his expression remained impassive. "Eighteen, maybe."

"Eighteen..." She considered the age. Eighteen meant high school and proms and starting college and voting for the very first time. Had she done these things already or were they still ahead of her? "What does eighteen feel like?"

He shrugged. "About the same as twenty does."

She tilted her head and looked at him. "You're twenty?"

"Yeah."

"Are you in college?" Even as the words came out, she knew the answer.

"Not me."

"Somehow I can't imagine you stuck doing research in some dusty library. You look too—" She hesitated. What he looked was strong and virile and extraordinarily physical, none of which she could say to him.

"I'm a bum," he said easily. "A gym rat."

"I beg your pardon?"

"Gym rat." He peppered the air with a few mock punches. "I pick up some money now and then fighting."

"I can't imagine why two men would want to climb into a ring and throw punches at each other."

"For money," he said, then shot her a dark look. "And because I like it."

She fell silent. Violence frightened her, and yet it didn't surprise her that he would choose a sport like that. "Can you make a living at it?"

"Hell, no."

"So what is it you do when you're not fighting?"

He grinned. "Fight some more."

"You're scaring me, Jack." That simmering anger she'd sensed in him from the start was almost visible in the shadowy hospital room. "Tell me the truth."

"You won't like it."

"Tell me anyway."

But he didn't. He made a quick, self-conscious joke and popped a mouthful of shivery green Jell-O into her mouth before she had a chance to protest. She tried to imagine him stripped to boxing trunks, sweating beneath the lights in some cheap gym in Sunnyside or the West Side of Manhattan while he dodged the punches thrown by an aging prizefighter with more muscles than brains.

The thought of Jack reduced to such barbaric terms made her sad, and she looked down at her tray and blinked away the tears forming in her eyes. Had she always been this foolish, this sloppily sentimental, or was this another result of her accident, the same as the lacerations and broken bones?

"Hey, don't cry," he said, wiping the tears away with the back of his strong, tanned hand. "Jell-O isn't that awful, is it?"

"Yes, it is," she said, forcing herself back from the abyss of questions. "I bet you'd cry too if you had to eat this."

His chest puffed out in a caricature of male swagger. "Nothing makes me cry."

Her eyes widened. "Really?"

"It takes a heart to cry." He thumped his chest. "They say I don't have one."

"Everyone has one."

"Not me." He thumped his chest again. "Hear the echo?" he asked with a smile. "Nothing in there."

He was trying to make her laugh. She understood that, but the sadness in his eyes made those traitorous tears reappear. "You have a heart, Jack," she whispered. "I'm proof of that."

"You're proof of nothing," he said gruffly. "Maybe I was just looking for a reward."

"No." She met his eyes, let him see her tears the same as he'd seen her laughter. "You did it because you're a good man."

He tried to turn away from her, but the truth was such a powerful force that not even a man as strong as Jack could fight it.

"Don't make me out to be some kind of hero," he mumbled. "I just—" He stopped and her heart ached as he searched for words.

Mary wanted to help him, to give him the words he needed to express himself, but a flood of emotion choked off her voice. She clung to his hand as if it were a lifeline, marveling that so strong a man could be so shaken by an act of kindness. Her heart soared with the realization that the bond between them was as real as the air she breathed. She hadn't imagined the intensity of their connection or embroidered the depth of his need for her.

Jack might have pulled her from the burning car but somehow she'd saved his life. Mary was as certain of that one fact as she was uncertain of her own past.

"I saw you," he said, looking down at their joined hands, his face hidden from her eyes. "I was waiting for the light to change at the corner by the Plaza, and I saw you pull up in the li—in the car." He looked up, an expression of awe and wonder in his dark eyes.

She felt as if she were being pulled straight into his soul.

"You were the most beautiful thing I'd ever seen in my life." His words came fast and eloquent. "I wanted to run over to the car, to get closer to you, to—"

"Go ahead," Mary whispered. "Tell me, please."

He raked a hand through his hair and grimaced. "Damn, it sounds so stupid now." He drew a deep breath. "I wanted to see if you were real, if I'd imagined you, because only an angel could look the way you did."

He spoke of innocence, of purity. He spoke from loneliness and need, and he reached past Mary's fear and her pain and touched her heart. Had anyone else ever felt that way about her? Would anyone ever again?

"I dodged the traffic. Hell, I was no more than ten feet away from the car when you turned and looked at me."

"I did?" She struggled for memory but there was none.

"You smiled and turned away again, and I just stood there staring at you and then it...the taxi..." He lowered his head, and her eyes filled with tears at the sight of his huge shoulders shaking. "I thought you were gone. I wanted to curse God for hurting you, for not letting one beautiful thing live in this stinking world, when I saw you through the window and—"

"And you rescued me." She touched his cheek with her hand, wishing she were hale and whole and able to soothe him with an embrace. "You did what nobody else had the guts to do, Jack. You saved my life."

"I had to. If anybody in this world deserved a chance, it was you."

"You don't even know me."

"Doesn't matter. I know all I need to know about you."

Her laughter surprised them both. "Then would you please tell me who I am?"

"I'd do anything for you," he said, "but I don't know if I could do that."

Warmth spread up from the soles of her feet, through her shattered limbs, pooling in her midsection and chest. "I'll remember sooner or later. The doctors have promised me this is temporary."

"And after you remember? Then what?"

"I—I don't know. Maybe I have family somewhere or friends—"

"You have me."

She tried to look away, but his gaze was too compelling. "Don't, Jack. Don't say things you don't mean because I just might believe you."

He dropped to his knees next to the hospital bed and brought his face—that beautiful, broken face—next to hers. His eyes were the dark blue of a summer night sky; they seemed to darken with emotion as he looked at her.

"I can take care of you." His voice was low and fierce. "I'll keep you safe."

"How can you?" she cried, wishing it could be so. "You have no money. Your mother already has more than she can handle. It's just a dream, Jack. A wonderful dream that can't come true."

"I'll make it come true."

"How?" she said again. "Short of robbing a bank, you can't—" She stopped, cold inside at the subtle change of expression in his eyes. "Dear God," she whispered, "don't even think of it."

"I could do it. I *would* do it for you."

"You'd ruin your life. It's wrong, Jack. Terribly wrong." Her memory had vanished, but her sense of morality had not.

"It's wrong that you don't have anyone," he said, voice rising with anger. "It's wrong that those bastards on Park Avenue have more money than they can count. It's wrong that you're in this place alone."

"I'm not alone." She reached for his arm, but he danced out of reach. *Dear God, let me say the right thing. Don't let him do anything crazy....* "I have you."

"You can have more."

"I'm alive." She forced a smile. "Doesn't that count for something, Jack?"

He looked at the equipment lining the wall of the hospital room, the cast on her arm and her leg, and the bandages everywhere. "This is as good as it gets, sweetheart. Without money, you'll be in that bed the rest of your life."

He's right ... he's right... "I don't care. You don't go out and rob a bank because life is unfair."

His rage filled the room. She found it difficult to breathe as she watched him pace like a caged lion. "There's no other way. Nobody gives you nothing in this world. You gotta go out and take what you need."

"You're scaring me, Jack."

He stopped but didn't turn to face her. He leaned against the window, head resting against the woodwork. Silhouetted by the late afternoon sun, his muscular body stood out in sharp relief against the white hospital walls. So much rage to carry around—what Mary wouldn't give to ease his pain the way he'd eased hers.

I've never wanted for money. The thought came as suddenly as the calm after a storm. *I've never wanted for anything my whole life.* She'd been cared for and protected and safe her entire life, and there was nothing in her conscious or unconscious memory that could help her understand the angry young man who stood before her. They were worlds apart—lifetimes, maybe—and only an act of fate had brought them together. He had risked his life in the fire to save her from certain death. She had no doubt he would risk his freedom to give her back her health.

"I'm not your responsibility," she said, praying he would listen with both his mind and his heart. "You saved me. That's enough for one lifetime, isn't it?"

"Not for me." He met her eyes, and the love she saw in them both frightened her and filled her with joy. "You need someone. You need me."

And then she realized that her past might be well and truly gone. That whoever she was and whatever she'd been had died in the crash along with the others. Her old life was gone forever. If she did have family somewhere out there, how important was she to them if her absence wasn't even missed?

This was all there was, this moment in time, with only this savage and tender young man to stand between Mary and a dark void of loneliness that stretched farther than the eye could see or the mind could imagine.

"Stay with me," she whispered. "Don't ever leave me alone."

He was at her side in the space of a heartbeat. "I won't," he said, his breath warm against her cheek. "I'll never leave you."

And because she wanted to so very much, she believed him.

Geneva

THE MAN LOOKED UP as his young assistant entered the room. "I told you I didn't want to be disturbed."

"This is important," said the assistant, handing over a courier pouch. "From New York."

The man muttered an oath and withdrew a sheaf of papers. His trained eye skimmed the contents, then settled upon one small paragraph near the bottom of the second page.

Refolding the pages, he brought his attention back to his assistant. "It seems as if we are heading back to New York in the morning."

The young man's gingery eyebrows lifted a fraction. "They finally ID'd the limousine?"

"No. Our friends did a good job of destroying the numbers. They traced her through Sara Spencer. Five days," said the man with a shake of his head. "The

NYPD isn't as efficient as it once was." How clever of his niece to make her arrangements under another name to foil the press. He capped his Montblanc fountain pen and looked out his hotel room window at the stunning view of the Alps at twilight. He'd miss that view. "Remind me to reserve a suite here at Christmastime."

The assistant nodded and jotted something in his tiny leather-bound pad. "Do they—I mean, do they suspect—"

He had forgotten how powerful a man could feel with his hands wrapped around the throat of a younger, weaker man. "Say that one more time," he snapped into his assistant's ear, "or even think it, and..." He let the pressure of his fingers on the man's windpipe speak for him.

Red-faced and gasping, his assistant apologized profusely then backed out of the room to make reservations to New York.

This sudden departure would cause talk among the government types and technicians traveling with him, but he would take care of that with a few well-chosen words. Well-chosen words, after all, had carried him far in life—to this point in time where he could write "End" to it all.

At long last it was over. The father was dead. The senator. The Secretary's son. The girl might have proved troublesome, but according to his reports, her memory had disappeared the night of the crash. Perhaps Providence had watched over him after all. The girl had always held a special spot in his heart—after all, she was the last of the line and for that alone was important.

There had always been the chance that she didn't know of her new husband's suspicions. Now those suspicions were as dead as the people who had entertained them.

Ah, yes, he thought as he poured himself a tumbler of Scotch. *Simple plans are always the best.* Soon he would swoop down to carry the girl off to recover and look the hero in the bargain.

He settled back to watch darkness fall over Geneva.

Chapter Four

When Hugh Scott issued an order, everybody jumped. Everybody, that was, except Rydcr O'Neal.

Ryder O'Neal, part of Scott's Geneva retinue, groaned and buried his head under his goose-down pillow. It was still dark outside. Nobody got up while it was still dark.

"I'm talking to you, O'Neal," called his pal Joe Morgan. "Rise and shine. We're shipping out."

"Get stuffed," Ryder mumbled into the eiderdown quilt. This was Switzerland, land of skiing, après-skiing and dreaming about skiing. His job description didn't mention keeping farmers' hours.

"You got five minutes to hit the floor running."

"Go away!" Ryder called out to the operative on the other side of the door. "I'll skip the muesli today." He hated the chopped nuts and berries that passed as breakfast cereal in this very civilized country and longed for a crude—and American—plate of ham and eggs. The door to his chalet bedroom opened.

Joe Morgan's voice made Ryder wince. "The old man's called out the jet. We're heading back stateside."

Ryder opened one eye and glared up at the younger and more enthusiastic man. "Big Blue calling us home?" Big Blue was the diplomatic corps' current nickname for the president of the United States.

"Family business. The old man's niece is in the hospital."

"Mary Flynn?" Everyone knew Mary Flynn Scott. Hell, even Ryder, inveterate cynic, had felt a lump in his throat when the kid graduated high school a year or so ago. "What happened?" Her uncle, Hugh Scott, had been distraught that the World Congress on Peace had kept him from attending her nuptials, but the Scott devotion to public service was legendary. So what if Scott's happiness over the marriage seemed more than a bit forced to Ryder?

Joe's jovial face darkened. "Car wreck." He cleared his throat and Ryder felt himself tense. "On the way to the reception. Killed her husband, the maid of honor, the best man and the limo driver."

Ryder's oath was heartfelt. "What the hell happened?"

"Anybody's guess. The report said a cab careened into the intersection and took them out one-two-three."

Ryder swung his legs out of the bed and wrapped a sheet around his bare middle as his brain clicked into gear. He searched the floor and the nightstand for his clothes. "Why'd he wait so long to fly back?"

"He just found out."

"Gimme a break, Morgan. We know what's happening before it happens."

"Not this time."

Ryder listened to the story while he yanked on his pants and shirt then threw his things into a battered leather suitcase. "I can buy the amnesia," he said as Morgan followed him out of his room and down the curving staircase. "But I'm having a hell of a lot of trouble with the rest of the story."

"I saw the pictures," said Morgan. "What I can't believe is that she lived through it." Morgan shuddered. "Nothing left but a pile of hot metal. The ID plate was melted beyond recognition."

"How bad is she?" A vision of a smiling Mary Flynn Scott on the day of her high school graduation melted into a grotesque parody of her lovely face.

"Broken bones, cuts, that kind of thing."

"Her face?"

"Nothing permanent."

It wasn't much, considering the enormity of her loss, but Ryder was glad she at least had been granted that one gift.

They joined up with the rest of the Scott entourage at the airfield. Scott's score of advisors, secretaries and hangers-on milled about their employer's limousine, looking duly serious and grief-stricken. Ryder smiled at two of the younger—and prettier—secretaries and grunted a hello to Hugh Scott's right-hand man. Thomas Judd was known for his uncanny ability to turn international brickbats into bouquets for his boss. Thomas Judd was also known for his uncanny ability to turn his boss's triumphs into his own.

And Hugh Scott, former Ambassador to the Court of St. James's and current roving emissary in search of world peace, had had his share of triumphs. Devoted public servant. Loving husband. Sorrowful widower. Generous and loyal uncle who took Mary Flynn under his wing when her father died so unexpectedly that April morning in Camp David. The only living male issue of the once indestructible Scotts of Rhode Island.

The public loved him. The press worshiped at his feet. Even PAX, the international antiterrorist organization that had placed Ryder in his retinue to oversee the cryptographic equipment, held Scott in the highest regard.

Ryder hated the man's guts.

He didn't trust Hugh Scott. He didn't believe Scott's endless declarations of modesty and team spirit. Call it intuition; call it a guess. Whatever you called it, Ryder was gut-certain the illustrious Hugh Scott was no better than the rest of mankind—and probably worse than most.

Ryder watched as the man in question exited from his limousine, looking suitably drawn and concerned. He had no reason to think Scott held his niece in anything but the highest esteem and affection. Why then did the whole thing feel so wrong?

RYDER WAS STILL ASKING himself that question after the jet left Swiss airspace.

Hugh Scott had called him into the forward cabin to reconfigure a code so a particularly sensitive message could be relayed to the powers-that-be at the White House without fear of Soviet bloc interception. Ryder made the requisite noises about Mary Flynn's accident and found himself watching the older man carefully for signs of insincerity. There weren't any.

"She's young and strong," Scott had said, his snake-green eyes misting over with unshed tears. "Physically I'm certain she'll recover. But emotionally—" He shook his head sadly. "Emotionally, that's another story. That will take love of family to pull her through."

Perfect answer, thought Ryder as the jet streaked toward New York City. He'd replayed the answer over and over in his head and each time he analyzed it, he found it to be flawless. Cadence, intonation—hell, Scott's very choice of words. Perfect parts that added up to an all-too-perfect whole.

"Great guy," said Joe Morgan as Scott made his way through the press section of the jet, shaking hands and asking the reporters to pray for his "...dear sweet Mary..."

"Yeah," muttered Ryder. "Great guy."

"The guy's worried sick about the kid."

"Yeah," muttered Ryder again as Scott accepted a shot of Dewar's from a UP veteran. "He's all broken up about it."

Ryder was a cynic born-and-bred. He'd never bought into Santa Claus, the Easter Bunny or the Tooth Fairy. While his brothers and sisters were writing Christmas lists and leaving baby teeth under their pillows, Ryder was telling all who would listen that the Emperor had no clothes.

He'd suffered no childhood traumas, no unusual adolescent upheavals, that would make him cast such a baleful eye at mankind and its antics. He had simply been born with an uncommonly keen eye and sharp ear for the absurdities of life that made it possible for him to cut through the layers of bull and go straight to the heart of the matter.

While that ability didn't make him the most endearing cocktail party guest in town, it did make him one of PAX's most effective operatives.

Dirty job? *Send O'Neal. He won't bat an eyelash.*

Bomb ticking and only twenty seconds left before the big bang? *O'Neal has ice water in his veins and the steadiest hands in town.*

Looking to shatter illusions and destroy a few ideals? *O'Neal's your man. He has nothing to lose.*

What had happened to Mary Flynn Scott was a shame, but it had nothing to do with him.

Her uncle was a cultured sleaze, and that also had nothing to do with Ryder. He didn't have to like Hugh Scott in order to work for him.

His job for PAX was to keep the crypto equipment up and his ears open for any infiltration from the other side. Anything else was on his own time.

"THEY'RE GOING TO DO some tests," said Mary on the morning of the sixth day. "I won't be back in my room until after lunch."

"Okay," said Jack, stifling a yawn. "I'll be here."

Mary took a deep breath. "No."

His face darkened. "What do you mean 'no'?"

"I think you should get some rest."

"This is a hospital," he said, flashing her an exhausted grin. "I get plenty of rest right here."

She knew him well enough by now to know he wouldn't like what she was about to say. "I think you should go home, Jack."

The grin slid into a scowl. "Forget it."

"I'm serious. You've been with me for days. The head nurse told me you sleep in the hallway outside my door."

"Old lady talks too much," he muttered.

"You're asleep on your feet, Jack. I'm worried about you."

He flexed a muscle. "Strong and healthy. Just worry about getting better."

She opted for a different tactic. "What about your family? Don't they wonder where you are?"

His shrug was more eloquent than any words he could say. "I don't think anybody's even noticed I'm gone."

"I can't believe that," she whispered, her voice breaking with a surge of emotion. "You're a wonderful man."

His laugh was sharp, bitter. "You'd get one hell of an argument on that, sweetheart."

"Not from me."

He met her eyes and they looked at each other. The moment stretched past the point of comfort, then slid into dangerous territory. *You're a wonderful man, Jack,* she thought. *Why don't you believe it?*

The moment could have gone on forever but a tap at the door broke the spell. Two attendants breezed into the room with a stretcher. "Ready to go for a test drive?" the younger one asked, with a quick look in Jack's direction.

Mary nodded. "Ready."

The attendants lifted Mary and her paraphernalia onto the stretcher with one easy motion. Jack's sigh of relief seemed to surround her when she smiled up at him.

"Get some rest," she whispered to Jack as the attendants wheeled her out of the room.

He seemed to gather strength before her eyes. "I'll be here when you get back."

"Good," said Mary.

He brushed a kiss against her temple. "Go get 'em, tiger."

SHE WAS GETTING BETTER every day. Jack didn't need fancy tests to tell him that. It was the look in her eyes, the sound of her voice, the way she laughed when he told her the worst jokes he could think of.

She was definitely getting well and that meant he had to come up with some way to take care of her. As long as she was a Jane Doe, the city took care of her. New York City was tenderhearted in cases like this, but that tenderheartedness didn't last long.

He'd heard the rumors about relatives in high places. One smart-mouthed doctor said she was the daughter of a dead president. What a joke. She had no people. If she had, why would they let her rot in some hospital, all alone except for a bum like Jack? No, it was all pretty clear to him. He'd saved her life. She was his responsibility. He'd find a way to care for her.

The nurse disappeared onto the elevator with the attendants, and Jack approached the nurses' station. That redhead was on duty. He hated her. She had a way of looking through him as if he were six feet four inches of dirt.

He gestured toward the elevator. "How long are her tests gonna take?"

The nurse didn't even look up. "Who wants to know?"

He wanted to grab her by her starched white collar and force her to look at him, to *see* him, but he controlled himself. "Jack Flanagan."

She pursed her thin lips and continued scribbling something in her log book. *You know damn well who it is,* he thought as he struggled with his temper. *Just give me an answer.* He kept his eyes on her, almost smiling as she began to squirm under the intensity of his scrutiny. *Give up, lady. I'm not going away until I get an answer.*

He had to hand it to her: she hung in there longer than most men would have, but finally she looked up.

"Jane Doe?" she asked.

Jack nodded.

"I wouldn't go pacing the halls if I were you. She won't be back in her room until two or three."

He grunted a thanks and turned away before the red-haired nurse had a chance to let him know how insignificant he was in the scheme of things. He didn't need a stranger to tell him that when he had his family telling him he was worthless every day of his life. Hell, he did a pretty good job of that himself.

But right now none of it mattered. He didn't care what the red-haired nurse thought of him. He didn't give a damn about anything except the beautiful young girl who had handed him back his heart.

He would do anything to keep her safe from harm. Anything.

And it wasn't until he was halfway back to Brooklyn before he realized he didn't know where to begin.

"I DON'T LIKE HIM." Ryder O'Neal paced up and down the length of Alistair Chambers's Manhattan apartment two hours after landing at JFK. "Hugh Scott doesn't give a damn what happens to that girl. All he cares about is his public image."

Alistair said nothing. He took his time lighting his Gauloise and then took even longer exhaling a long, leisurely plume of smoke. "He's a politician, my boy. A certain selfishness goes with the territory."

"He's a cold-blooded SOB, if you ask me."

Alistair took another drag on his Gauloise. "I wasn't aware that I had."

"The girl's all alone," Ryder raged, "and Scott decided to hold a press conference before he left for the hospital."

"Scott has responsibilities."

"He has responsibilities to his niece."

"Isn't that being simplistic, Ryder? I haven't noticed an excessive amount of concern for your own nieces and nephews."

Going for the jugular, are you, Chambers? "My nieces and nephews have parents. Mary Flynn doesn't." There wasn't an American over the age of ten who didn't know the sad story of Mary Flynn Scott, who'd been orphaned upon her father's sudden death a few years back. How altruistic and loving Hugh Scott had looked when he took the young girl under his wing and whisked her off to his London apartment. How beautifully he had played the media for every ounce of good press.

"Perhaps this is the time to inject another pleasant reminder that you are paid to perform a service for PAX, not to become involved in Hugh Scott's family affairs."

"I bet if I ran a check on Scott I'd come up with a few savory tidbits that might make you sit up and take notice, Chambers." When in doubt, come out swinging.

Chambers laughed, but his laugh was more subdued. "I wouldn't bet my life savings on it."

"The guy's a sleaze. Self-serving, slippery. Cold as a snake and—"

"One of us."

Ryder's jaw dropped. "What did you say?"

Chambers wasn't laughing any longer. "I said, he is one of us."

"Define what you mean by 'one of us.'"

Chambers exhaled a plume of smoke. "He's a member of PAX."

"Okay," said Ryder, relaxing once again. "Very funny."

"Hugh Scott joined the organization just before the Bay of Pigs invasion, 1962. Currently inactive, but definitely still in."

"So much for the infallibility of PAX."

"Scott's done his share for us," said Chambers, watching Ryder closely.

"He's probably done more for himself."

Alistair lit another cigarette. "Do you care to tell me what exactly has brought about this outpouring of venom?"

"I don't like him."

"Not good enough," said Chambers. "You don't ruin a man because you don't care for his personality." The older man reached for his telephone. "Fenelli will take over your post."

Ryder stared at him in shock. "You're transferring me?"

"That seems the wisest move."

"I'm not finished with Scott yet."

"I'm afraid you are." Alistair pressed a series of numbers, paused, then pressed a longer series of numbers. He placed the phone back in its cradle and looked up at Ryder. "Take the rest of the week off, then report back to me for reassignment."

"What if I won't go?"

"You will." Alistair's expression was grave and steady. "You don't have a choice."

MARY WAS TIRED and sore by the time they wheeled her back into her room, but not so tired that she didn't immediately notice that Jack was gone. At first she was pleased to think that he'd taken her advice and gone home for a while to rest, but as it grew close to five o'clock, so did her anxiety.

"Don't be ridiculous," she said out loud to the empty room. "He has the right to go out for a while." Hadn't she encouraged him to do exactly that a few hours ago? She had told him he needed to go home and sleep, and she had meant every word she said, but she simply hadn't imagined how lonely she would feel without him. In less than a week that dark and threatening young man had become the focal point of her existence. Indeed, he was the sole reason that she was alive.

It was the dream, she told herself, trying to concentrate on the television news blaring from the set suspended in the corner of the room. *That's why you're feeling so jumpy.* Last night she had refused a sleeping pill and instead of deep, dreamless sleep, she struggled through a succession of hazy dreams, peopled by shadowy figures who all seemed familiar. Once she was approached by a handsome young man in formal dress; he held out his hands to her in supplication. In the dream Mary had tried desperately to reach him but was awakened by her own sobs before she reached his outstretched hands.

Jack was next to her in an instant, soothing her, comforting her, holding her close to his broad, hard chest until she drifted back into sleep again. It was a foolish dream—she knew that. Her subconscious playing tricks on her. But the sensation of loss, of abandonment, still lingered, and it was heightened now without Jack by her side.

Her memory was coming back. Although she had admitted that to no one, she knew it was true, and the thought terrified her. The handsome young man in the tuxedo from her dream was important to her. The pain she felt when she awoke and found herself without him had been too intense to dismiss. When she tried to nap, images flickered across her closed lids like a silent movie. The smell of roses . . . bright lights and loud voices . . . a deep voice rich with promise . . .

"I don't want to know." The sound of her own voice triggered no stream of memories, but the sound of a nurse laughing in the hallway made her think of a summer picnic in a shady glen.

There was danger in these memories. Each one was another piece in the puzzle of who and what she was, bringing her nearer to the truth. She struggled to stay awake, to keep the dreams away. She wanted to stay right there, safe and protected within the four white walls of her hospital room with Jack to protect her.

She felt so vulnerable without him. He gave shape to her days, forcing the amorphous hours of her day into form and pattern, casting light into the dark corners of her heart. Without him there next to her, the nurses seemed threatening, their chatter fraught with doublespeak. The crackling sound of the loudspeaker, the false cheer from doctors who clearly resented the fact that their fancy medicines couldn't coax her memory out from hiding.

Little did they know her memory was reawakening, filling her with confusion and fear and an overwhelming desire to bury her face in Jack's broad chest and stay there forever. That sharp burst of heartache she'd experienced when Jack told her she was the only survivor of the car crash was only the beginning. If she let herself remember, it would all come back, grabbing her by the throat and choking the breath out of her until she finally sank into the same oblivion Jack had saved her from.

The opening music from 'Eyewitness News' blared from the television in the corner and she fumbled around for the remote control. "Political circles are buzzing about roving ambassador Hugh—"

The gray-haired head nurse darted into the room and clicked off the television. "Nothing but bad news today, honey," she said briskly, her eyes darting away from Mary's own. "Besides, you have yourself a visitor."

"Jack isn't a visitor," Mary said with a soft laugh. "He doesn't have to be announced." *Something's wrong,* a voice whispered. *Something's terribly wrong.*

The nurse sat down on the edge of the bed and took Mary's hand in her own. "It isn't Jack, honey."

Mary's heart thudded painfully against her rib cage. "Did he call? Do you think something happened to him?"

"The boy is fine. He probably went home and fell asleep." Her smile was bittersweet. "He's been in overdrive since the day they brought you in."

"I wanted him to go home and rest." Mary lifted her chin and met the nurse's gaze. "He deserves it." She heard footsteps in the hall by her door, and she talked quickly to hide her nervousness. "He was so sleepy this morning that I made him go down to the cafeteria and drink a pot of coffee. I told him he should—"

"Honey, your uncle is outside."

"I told Jack he should make sure he—"

The nurse placed a finger against Mary's lips. "Your name is Mary, honey. Your family is here for you."

"No!"

"Don't be afraid," said the nurse, stroking Mary's hair. "You have people who love you, people who will help you recover your past."

"No!" Mary's voice grew louder, more shrill. "I want Jack."

"Jack isn't here, Mary. Your uncle wants to see you."

"I don't have an uncle." She couldn't stop the tears from coursing down her cheeks. "I don't have anybody but Jack."

"Your name is Mary Flynn Scott," said the nurse, her own eyes glistening. "Your father was Frederick Scott. He was President of the United States."

"Now I know you're kidding!" Her laugh tore at her throat and bounced off the white walls of her hospital room. "Did Jack put you up to this? Are you related to him? Is this a joke?" *Of course it is! Jack's right out there in the hall, smiling, looking to make me laugh....*

"You were married, Mary."

"I don't want to hear this."

"You married William Pennington one week ago."

"No," Mary whispered, slipping toward the darkness. *This is true...my father...my husband...Jack, where are you? Don't let me remember this....* "Please, no."

"Oh, honey." The nurse kissed Mary's cheek then stood up. "Let me bring your uncle in. Let him tell you."

It's true...it's true...it can't be...why aren't you here, Jack? Please come back before it's too late....

"Mary."

She looked up. A tall man in a gray suit stood in the doorway. A man with green eyes and a square jaw and a face so like her father's that it hurt to look at him.

"Do you know me, Mary?"

She nodded, too frightened and too in pain to speak. Her father—so tall, so strong, so wonderful. He was dead now, wasn't he?

"You're going to be fine, Mary," the man said as he strode across the room to sit by her bed. "I've come to take care of you."

"Jack," she said, her voice soft at first. "I want Jack."

"Listen to me, Mary. You've had a terrible accident, but the doctors tell me you'll be fine. You're ready to be moved."

Where was the nurse? Why wasn't she there? The nurse could explain to Mary's uncle why she didn't want to leave. As long as she was there in her hospital room, she was safe.

As long as she was there, she had Jack. He loved her. She knew he loved her. He'd pulled her back from that bright light, held her in his arms, made her feel safe and whole and—

"...believe me," her uncle continued, his voice deep and commanding, "time heals all wounds. You're young. You'll get over your loss."

"I don't want to hear this."

"I know it's difficult, Mary Flynn, but you aren't the first young woman to be widowed."

"Don't say it! I don't want you to say it." *Now, Jack! Put your arms around me before I break apart.* "Nobody asked you to come here. Leave me alone!" *...the back seat of a white limousine...the smell of roses all around her...her husband's smile as he whispered...* "Oh dear God!" The scream ripped apart her soul. "Billy's dead!"

"IT'S GOING TO WORK," Jack said out loud as he rode the empty elevator up to Mary's room on the fourth floor. "It's gotta work."

He couldn't move her into the apartment with Ma and Katherine. Between the stink of booze and Katherine's endless silence, he and the girl wouldn't stand a chance in hell of making a go of it. He wouldn't abandon them but neither would he tie himself up with their needs and anger any longer. His whole life he'd done nothing but wait for it to be his turn and that time had finally come.

No more watching other people be happy. No more cursing God for making him a bum from Brooklyn. No more wondering when it would start to get better. He'd found them a place where he and the bride could be happy.

His time was now. He would do whatever it took to make a life for the girl and keep his family from destroying itself. He'd sweep floors or dig ditches—he'd do anything to make this dream come true. She belonged to him. He'd never let her down.

The elevator doors slid open, and he stepped out into the brightly lit hallway. He walked tall, filled with a purpose for the first time in his life. A long time ago he had stopped believing in God, in goodness and a greater purpose. There was nothing in his life to prove otherwise.

Now he knew better. That someone like the girl could exist in this stinking world was proof enough for him that sometimes when you least expected it, God took care of His own.

His favorite nurse, the one from Hell's Kitchen, was off duty. He couldn't wait to tell the nurse tomorrow that he'd figured out a way to take care of the girl.

Just before he reached her door, he stuck his hand into the pocket of his jeans and withdrew a ring of keys. Her dark blue eyes would widen, then she'd laugh, and he'd lean over, and she'd place a kiss on his cheek, and he'd—

The room was empty.

He stepped inside, heart pounding. *Okay, don't worry. So she isn't back from the tests yet. No reason to get paranoid, is there?* The keys slipped from his hand, and he wiped the sweat onto the leg of his jeans, then picked them up from the floor.

The bed was made, the white sheets tucked tightly around the mattress. The pillow was fluffed. Everything was perfect, waiting for his girl to return.

But she wasn't going to. He knew that straight through to his gut. The room smelled of disinfectant and soap. The monitors were gone. The pitcher of water that rested on her nightstand was empty and tucked neatly into a corner of her dresser.

He turned and two seconds later skidded to a stop in front of the nurses' station.

"Where is she?" he demanded of the evening supervisor.

She met his eyes. He would always like her for that. "They released her."

His legs started to tremble. He couldn't let them see a sign of weakness. "When?"

She didn't blink. "One hour ago."

Blood thundered in his ears as the anger throbbed to life. "A letter," he said, leaning over the counter. "A note. Something. She must have left something."

The nurse sifted through the papers scattered on her desk. Her face was pale but two bright patches of red stained her cheeks and her hands trembled. "I'm sorry. Nothing."

"Who took her? Where did she go?" *You're losing it, Flanagan. She's scared. You can't get any answers if she's scared.* But it was so hard to control the pain, so hard to rein in the years of anger threatening to explode.

"Her uncle came for her. I don't know where he's taken her."

This wasn't the end. It couldn't be. She wouldn't have left him like that, without a note or a phone number. Something. Their bond was too strong. He wasn't crazy. He hadn't imagined the strong pull between them, a pull that turned death into life. A pull that turned a dead-end life into something wonderful.

She wouldn't.

He vaulted the low counter and pushed the nurse aside. Prescriptions. Records. Letters and magazines and calendars. He searched through everything then sent the rejects scattering across the floor.

The nurse was talking to him. Her voice was low, soothing, the sound of a professional trying her best to keep the savage in line. He heard the words; he recognized them; but he had travelled so far from that place, that moment, that her words couldn't reach him. A red mist of rage clouded his vision and clogged his brain as the enormity of his loss hit him square in the gut.

What a fool he'd been to think his life could ever be any different.

Twenty years of being on the wrong side of every good thing life had to offer pressed against his brain and ripped at his heart, and he turned to the one thing that had never failed him: his fists.

With a primitive roar of pain, he set out to destroy everything in his sight.

PART II

Chapter Five

Today

Hot. There was no doubt in anybody's mind that sultry night in June: Flynn was the hottest thing around.

She stood poised at the top of the staircase leading down to her ringside seats at the Trump Castle Hotel on Paradise Island and smiled for the cameras. She was aware of the picture she made—and exactly how much that picture would bring the lucky photographer.

"Flynn! Baby, turn this way."

"Give us some teeth, Flynn! Got me a mortgage to make."

Flashbulbs popped like gunfire. She aimed her thousand watt special model's smile into the bright white lights. She loved the camera as much as it loved her. She loved creating herself anew each time she faced the lens. She loved the openness and the mystery; the way her body managed to hide her soul. If only it could help her forget the wail of an ambulance siren…the sting of metal and glass…the sterile white walls of her hospital room and—

"Bring your notebook, Flynn?"

She turned to see Stanley Moses, managing editor of *Sports Weekly*, standing behind her with an entourage of eager underlings. *Sports Weekly* had offered to fly her to Paradise Island for the fight, provided she would write an article on the championship bout. Not that anyone cared if she could string subject and verb together, mind you; her article would appear in their brand-new let's-beat-*Sports Illustrated*-to-the-punch swimsuit issue, complete with a six-page spread of Flynn posing in microbikinis on a stretch of Brazilian beach.

"Don't worry, Stanley," she said with the carefree laugh that had sold everything from sex to soap powder. "You'll get your money's worth."

"Management is afraid you glamour girls can't spell."

"I'll turn in a Pulitzer prize-winning essay or I'll eat your hat." No matter that she'd never written more than a thank-you note in her life. When you were as famous as Flynn, it really didn't matter. They were buying the package, not the product this time.

"Not until I get my new hair weave." Stanley Moses gave his baseball cap an extra tug, and his employees looked away to hide their grins. "Mind if I sit with you?"

Flynn shrugged her bare shoulders in a whisper of silk and Obsession. "Not unless something better comes along." With a grin and a pinch of Stanley's angular cheek, she started down the stairs toward her seat.

Better offers always came along. That was one of the things she'd learned along the way. While this wasn't the life she'd thought she'd live, it suited her purposes. The first year after the accident had been one of darkness and pain. She had railed at God, cursing the Almighty for taking her husband but sparing her life.

She would always be grateful to her Uncle Hugh for taking her to a hospital in Switzerland where both her body and spirit could be restored away from the relentless glare of the American press. His loving support had helped carry her through the darkest days. Somehow Hugh Scott had managed to keep it all private—her marriage to Billy, her identity, the sad and pointless end to all her girlish dreams. She never asked how he had managed such a feat, and he had never volunteered the information. It didn't matter. For two years, nothing had.

Her body mended. Her spirit took longer.

There were times when she cursed the dark-eyed boy who'd pulled her back from death. She couldn't put a face to the memory, but the feeling of being protected, of being loved, lingered today after all these years. How strange it was that while it grew harder to recall the precise sound of Billy's voice, the smell of his skin, she could still conjure up the feeling of security she had felt in the arms of her fierce protector. She had wanted to tell him how much he'd mattered to her, but by the time she emerged from her period of mourning, her uncle claimed to have forgotten what hospital she had been in. "Put it out of your mind, honey," he had said. "Get on with your life."

It bothered her to this day that she had never told the boy how much he meant to her.

"Time heals," they had told her as the weeks turned into months. At first she didn't believe them, for she was positive that the ache inside her heart would never disappear. But the months turned into years, the ache became bearable, and on her twenty-second birthday, she decided that since she hadn't died, it was time to get on with the business of living.

And so there she was, two months shy of her twenty-ninth birthday. Rich. Famous. Known for her face and not for her family. She had shed Mary Scott as if she had never existed. Flynn played with the right people, went to the right parties, appeared on the covers of all the right magazines. She had an apartment on the upper East Side of Manhattan, a beach house in the Hamptons, and a cottage in the Berkshires.

And she had men. Lots of them. Her beauty drew them to her; her mystery kept them interested. It didn't matter either way to Flynn. Her thoughts were fiercely sexual but her manner remained cool. A few had shared her body but no one had ever come close to touching her heart. Probably no one ever would.

Which was exactly the way Flynn wanted it.

"YOU'RE A MACHINE," said the small black man with a cigar clamped between his teeth. "You're a wrecking machine." He reached up and rubbed the younger man's shoulders. "You're gonna knock the bum out before he has a chance to tie on his gloves."

Wild Man Jack Flanagan turned around and held out his hands to be taped. "I'm a killing machine." He stared into his trainer's eyes. "I hope the bum said his prayers."

Oscar Davis ripped off a piece of tape and started wrapping Jack's hands. "You're going out on top, boy. You're going to show them all what a champ you are.''

Forty-two wins, eighteen knockouts, no losses. Jack had been at the top of the fight game for five years now. As undisputed heavyweight champion of the world, he had captured the world's imagination with his particular brand of down and dirty street fighting combined with a physical presence that Madison Avenue hucksters and TV talk-show hosts found equally unbeatable. The fact that he had been able to keep clean in a notoriously Mob-dominated sport generated as much press ink as his boxing skills did.

Because he knew how to use his fists—and because he didn't mind having his body used as a punching bag in the early days—he was a millionaire. Mom and his sister Katherine were tucked away in a mansion in northern New Jersey, complete with hot and cold running servants and their own private lake. His brothers and other sisters were set up for life. He bought them houses, paid their bills, made sure their kids went to the best schools and drove the flashiest cars.

He was a soft touch. A champ in the ring but a first-class chump once the spotlight faded. Money had turned out to be a great way to make friends and influence people. Reporters liked him. Cabdrivers and construction workers and the man on the street took his success as their own. A kid from the streets of Bed-Stuy who made it out and into the Big Time. Women found the bad boy image irresistible. Danger, after all, was the ultimate turn-on. Rich, tired businessmen got their kicks hanging out with a man who made his living with his fists and partied as if there was no tomorrow.

Because for Jack there wasn't a tomorrow. Tomorrow the fighting would be over. The spotlights would go out.

And he would have to figure out what to do with the rest of his life.

"Flynn." Donald Trump, owner of the casino/hotel, extended his tanned hand. "You're looking splendid, as usual."

Flynn smiled at America's most visible billionaire and shook his hand. "So are you, Donald."

"I'm glad you decided to come. This will be an exciting fight." He motioned toward his beautiful blond wife who was greeting guests at the opposite side of the ring. "Hollywood says Wild Man could be the next Sly Stallone."

The analogy did nothing for her. She tended to like men with initials after their name, men who talked about foreign policy and deficit spending and left the glitter and glamour to her.

Trump moved on to speak to Henry Kissinger. Everyone who was anyone was packed into the huge arena. Two rows back Princess Stephanie cuddled with her heavy metal boyfriend who wore the same black leather jumpsuit Flynn had modeled in last month's *Vogue*. Across the aisle Kim Basinger passed a glass of champagne over to Mel Gibson who gallantly held it to the lips of Elizabeth Taylor.

Camera crews from eleven countries jockeyed for position around the huge boxing ring in front of her. The ring was cordoned off with thick ropes that she prayed kept the Neanderthal prizefighters on their side of the divider. The last thing she wanted was to have some mindless pugilist come flying over the rope and—

"Hey! Great seats." Stanley Moses settled himself down next to Flynn in the second row while his underling scrambled for standing-room-only spots. "Close enough to see them sweat."

Flynn shuddered. "Is it too late to back out of this assignment?"

Stanley eyed her from beneath the bill of his baseball cap. "Have you cashed your check yet?" Flynn nodded. "Then it's too late."

"Slave driver."

He took another look at her. "Am I crazy or weren't you a blonde yesterday?"

She laughed and her mane of auburn hair slid over her shoulders. "Revlon needed a redhead this morning, Stanley, and I aim to please."

He pulled an unpleasant face. "That stuff washes out, doesn't it?"

"Don't worry," she said, patting his arm. "I'll be blond again for the publicity photos." Truth was, she'd be blond again tonight when she washed her hair, but why let a man like Stanley know how easy it was to be beautiful?

The crowd erupted into cheers as an array of nubile young women—clad in white satin hot pants, skimpy halter tops and spike heels—climbed into the ring. They gave the term "dressed for success" a whole new meaning. A leering man with a gray walrus mustache handed each girl a placard and received a kiss on the cheek in return.

Laughing, she turned toward Stanley Moses, only to find his attention riveted to the spectacle before them.

"IBM," said Flynn, reading company names as they bounced past her seat. "Apple, AT&T—what is this, Moses? The battle of the Fortune 500 Bimbos?"

It seemed to take a full minute for Stanley to close his mouth and wipe away the drool. "They're sponsoring the event, Flynn."

She stared at him. "Why?"

He stared at her as if she had three Day-Glo orange heads. "Why?" he parroted. "Who wouldn't want their name attached to the fight of the decade?"

Flynn's laugh rang out above the cheering of the crowd. "Considering this is only 1990, that isn't saying much, Stanley."

"I'm disappointed in you." He cast a quick glance at the parade of beauties in the ring. "You need an attitude adjustment, Flynn. Maybe I shouldn't have given you the assignment, after all."

"Too late," she reminded him. "I cashed the check. Remember?"

The crowd was chanting something incomprehensible as the theme song from *Rocky* blared out from every loudspeaker in the arena. So much for ambience. She got down to work. "A cloud of smoke hangs over the ring like a thick gray atomic blast," she said into the tape recorder she'd tucked into her bag.

"Similes?" Stanley asked with an arched brow.

"Don't worry," she said, suppressing a grin. "I don't charge extra." She turned back to the tape recorder. "The place smells of suntan lotion, Cuban cigars, and money."

"Not bad," said Stanley, ignoring a bouncy red-head whose placard extolled the virtues of Gulf & Western.

A dark-haired man in a tuxedo climbed through the ropes then strode toward the center of the ring. The man in the tuxedo snapped his fingers and waited as a microphone was lowered from a cable suspended overhead, somewhere hidden in the thick gray smoke. Flynn had to admit the theatrics of the event were impressive. She half-expected a host of bikini-clad angels to descend from the heavens to preach the gospel according to Howard Cosell.

"Good evening, ladies and gentlemen, and welcome to the beautiful Trump Castle Hotel and Casino. We're proud to bring you the fight of the decade, the match of the century, the most important pugilistic event in the record annals of sport: the last fight ever for Wild Man Flanagan!"

The crowd screamed their approval. Flynn didn't even try to compete with them; she just let the tape recorder capture it all.

"This is great!" Stanley Moses screamed over the cheering of the crowd. "What a way to retire!"

Flynn moved the tape recorder between the two of them. "I admit it's impressive, but what if he loses?"

"Wild Man never loses," Stanley said.

"Everyone loses sometime."

"Don't let anybody else hear you say that."

"The man's a boxer, Stanley, not a statesman. I have the feeling you left your journalistic objectivity back home with Joanie and the kids."

"The guy's going places," he said, not cracking a smile. "Rumor has it he might run for public office."

Flynn laughed so hard she almost dropped her tape recorder. "I have a little experience in these matters, Stanley, and somehow I don't think the world is ready for a president who was heavyweight champion of the world."

"Don't be too sure," he said with a self-confident grin. "We elected a B-movie actor to the White House, didn't we?"

"GOOD LUCK, Wild Man!"

"Way to go, Flanagan. I got my money ridin' on you."

"Hey, man. Make sweet music with your fists...."

Jack barely heard the encouragements called out to him as he followed Oscar out of the dressing room and headed down the long corridor toward the entrance to the arena. He was only vaguely aware of the deafening chorus of boos rocking the building.

"Must've introduced Lenny," said his trainer with a short laugh. "Poor guy won't know what hit him."

"He'll know," said Jack, visualizing his fists making contact with his opponent's face. "He'll know exactly what hit him."

A cannonball. A torpedo. An irresistible force meeting a moveable object. He'd been called superhuman, a one-man death squad, the most powerfully agile boxer to come along since Muhammad Ali in his prime. And Jack was all of those things and one other: he was tired.

The blood lust that had started it all was gone. He no longer needed the money or the adulation or the sheer thrill of leather against bone. Outside the ring, he even liked Lenny Curtis.

Jack was at the top. He still had his looks and he still had his brains, and if he intended to hold on to both of them, the time to get out was now.

Oscar had done his job well: the corridor was dark and long and empty. A phalanx of security guards kept the throng of reporters and hangers-on from following them.

"You're the best," said Oscar, walking backward and fixing Jack with his eagle-eyed stare. "You're the best there ever was."

"I'm the best," said Jack, letting the words sink in and become fact. "Nobody can touch me."

"You'll drop him in five."

"Hell," said Jack, stabbing the air with lightning-quick jabs of his right fist, "I'll drop him in three."

"Lead with your left. Let him get in a few shots then bring in the heavy artillery."

"I'll be out of there before I can work up a sweat."

"Don't go gettin' too cocky, boy," Oscar warned as they reached the entrance to the arena. "I'm too old to be watching you showboat out there. Just drop him clean and easy. This ain't the time to be cute."

Jack looked at the man who had been father and mentor and friend to him for the past eight years. "It's gonna be all aces from here on in, Oscar. We got it made."

Oscar blinked quickly then scowled up at Jack. "Just win the fight, kid. Then we'll talk."

Oscar straightened the belt on Jack's black satin robe, tightened the laces of the boxing gloves.

"Ready?"

Jack made the sign of the cross and nodded. "Let's party."

SHE HAD SAT THROUGH endless introductions of judges and dignitaries, pirates and kings, and finally an angelic-looking referee whose silver hair glittered in the TV lights like the real thing. Her patience for sports minutiae was wearing thin and the fact that the theme song from *Rocky* was beginning to sound good to her was a sign she was in deep trouble.

"They've finally turned down the music," Flynn said into the tape recorder, "and they're dimming the lights." A deep rumbling bass drum sounded. Her fillings vibrated, and she heard the distinct sound of ten thousand people holding their collective breath.

The emcee gestured grandly toward the center aisle. "In the red trunks, ex-heavyweight champion, Olympic gold medal winner, Lenny 'Killer' Curtis."

Flynn stared as the fighter and his entourage swept their way up the aisle toward the ring. Curtis had to be the largest human being she had ever seen. He shrugged off the red satin robe with "Killer" embroidered across the back in flowing white script and mugged for the crowd. His head had been shaved bald, and his black skin gleamed in the spotlight.

"They're cheering for him," Flynn said to Stanley Moses. "I thought Wild Man was the favorite."

"He is," said Stanley, whistling and cheering along with the rest of the crowd. "Just wait."

Killer Curtis played to the audience for a few minutes, shadowboxing, waving at familiar faces, smiling for the cameras that seemed to be everywhere. "He seems happy," said Flynn, amazed. The man was about to punch and be punched for the next hour and he was laughing. Still photographers battled television news crews for space around the perimeter of the ring, and one enterprising camerawoman scaled the shoulders of a security guard for a close-up shot of the contender.

The crowd rose with one movement and turned toward the back. Flynn stood up and strained to see over the sea of perfectly coiffed heads. She kicked off her spike heels and scrambled up onto her seat, one hand on Stanley's shoulder, one hand clutching the tape.

"Some things have to be seen to be believed. The back doors are parting like the Red Sea and—damn!" She lost her footing and stumbled against Stanley.

"Get down," said her knight in shining armor. "If you break your leg, I'm not helping you until the fight's over."

"Nice guy," Flynn muttered, clambering off the seat. But then what could she expect from a man whose idea of a good time was watching two other men beat each other's brains out?

She didn't need to see him to know exactly where Wild Man was. The roar of excitement grew louder as he approached, almost as if he were visiting royalty. Stanley jammed two fingers in his mouth and let loose with a roof-rattling whistle. The editor of *Sports Weekly* was turning into a middle-aged boxing groupie before her very eyes.

"The man travels with the 1st Cavalry," Flynn shouted into the tape recorder. "Eisenhower had fewer lackeys with him on D-Day. This is the most ridiculous spectacle since *Ben-Hur*." She had come to the fight as a lark. Models were asked for their bra sizes more often than their opinions; the chance to be paid for her thoughts was too irresistible.

Not that anyone cared, mind you. What she did in front of the camera was of a great deal more interest to the public than anything she could possibly do away from the camera. Oh, there had been a brief—mercifully brief—flurry of interest in her past when she returned to public life a few years ago, but daughters of ex-presidents don't make interesting copy unless their last name is Kennedy. Her father had died a tragic but quiet death. No fallen warrior. No shooting star blazing across the horizon. Mary Flynn Scott had been his standard-bearer for a brief time after his death; the American public embraced her then soon forgot her. Public love affairs had a shorter life span than a butterfly.

And that was fine with Flynn. She had no family any longer, save for Uncle Hugh. She had learned to make her own way in this world and that was how she liked it. Smile for the camera, cash the obscenely large paychecks and keep one step ahead of your heart.

The roar of the crowd reached an ear-splitting crescendo as Wild Man passed within twenty feet of where Flynn and Stanley Moses were sitting. A black satin robe could look a trifle precious on a man, but there was nothing precious at all about the way it strained across Wild Man Flanagan's powerful shoulders. Flynn had seen a number of glorious male physiques in her day—men who modeled swim trunks tended to be built along impressive lines—but this Neanderthal boxer promised to be quite a splendid sight.

She wanted to reach out and lower the hood that obscured his face, but he walked swiftly past them— or as swiftly as a man surrounded by a score of uniformed security guards could possibly walk. She had the distinct feeling his private police force would have taken a dim view of such an act. Where Flynn had expected voluptuous Vegas show girls with feathered headpieces and spangled bikinis, she found sober men in uniform who eyed the crowd with suspicion. Flanagan walked alone except for the small and wiry black man who kept pace alongside him.

"I don't get it." She watched Wild Man's back as he climbed into the ring then turned to Moses. "I thought he'd have a slew of hangers-on."

"Not Wild Man's style," said Stanley. "The higher up he's climbed, the leaner his operation."

"I thought boxing was all show biz."

"Flanagan gives them a damn good show once the bell rings, not before. Killer Curtis is a three-ring circus."

Flynn glanced up at the black man in one corner and the white man in the other. Both men had their backs to her. So much for having terrific seats. "Is Flanagan the Great White Hope, then?"

The look Stanley Moses shot her was one of pure disgust. "Race doesn't have one damn thing to do with it." He quickly explained that both Wild Man's and Killer's appeal transcended race and prejudice. They were true sports phenomena: colorless in the best possible sense of the word. "Don't you get it, Flynn? What we have here is the ultimate conflict: two champions fighting their last bout. Only one can be the winner."

Wild Man shrugged out of his silk robe. His body was beautifully made, a Renaissance sculpture come to life beneath the spotlights, all rippling muscle and power at command. He acknowledged the audience then turned to speak to his trainer, and Flynn's breath caught as she noticed the network of scar tissue webbing his broad back. An odd chill rushed through her body. What on earth had caused those marks on his otherwise perfect torso? She leaned over to ask Stanley about the scars when the referee uttered a few magic words and the bell rang.

The two fighters circled each other warily. The ring was set a good six feet above the crowd, and with the rest of the arena plunged into darkness, there was something almost surreal about the play of spotlight and shadow across the canvas. It was no wonder that across the aisle Leroy Neiman scribbled furiously in his sketchbook. The contrasts of light and dark were mesmerizing.

She was about to tell Stanley that the whole thing reminded her of an exhibit of Helmut Newton's photographs that she'd seen at MOMA last autumn when it happened.

"Oh, my God!" Flynn leaped to her feet as Wild Man Flanagan's head snapped back with Killer Curtis's punch. "He's been hit!"

Chapter Six

"Sit down, Flynn!" Stanley Moses grabbed her wrist and pulled her back into her seat. "You're embarrassing me."

She stared, wide-eyed, as the referee took a good look at Wild Man then backed away so the fight could continue. Flanagan's lips were drawn back in a grotesque line by the mouthpiece and already his left cheek looked swollen and bruised. There was something primitive about his face, something so intensely masculine that she felt both drawn and repulsed simultaneously. Why on earth did that dual emotion feel so familiar?

Considering the nature of prizefighting, it seemed ridiculous to be surprised by the violence, but there it was. Knowing two men were going to exchange blows was one thing; actually seeing it was something else. And who would have imagined the gut-wrenching sound of leather against bone, or the groans or the—

Flanagan landed a solid blow to Lenny's body and the smaller man doubled up. Flanagan danced around his opponent; Wild Man's movements were incongruously graceful for a man his size. Lenny staggered then recovered. The audience was on its feet, screaming encouragements to the two fighters. Flynn's stomach tilted alarmingly.

By the middle of Round Three, Flynn was certain she was about to be ill. The heat . . . the smoke-filled air . . . the deafening noise . . . and, dear God, the unabashed, raw power of the fight—she sank down into her seat and buried her face in her hands. It wasn't as if she was unsophisticated. She understood the notion of controlled violence inherent in most sports. Compared to pro football, boxing was almost a walk in the park.

Her head understood. Her heart was another story. Each time Lenny landed a blow against Flanagan's granite jaw, she had to bite her lip to keep from crying out. Ridiculous to feel that way—both men were paid obscenely well for the pleasure of being knocked senseless. But there was an intensity about Flanagan that unnerved Flynn, though for the life of her she couldn't imagine why. After tonight, he would be nothing more than cocktail conversation, an interesting anecdote to trot out at one of the endless dinner parties that occupied her time.

"Is this normal?" she asked Stanley Moses during the lull between Rounds Four and Five. "This is taking forever."

"The heat getting to you?"

She nodded. It certainly wouldn't do to tell the editor who'd given her the assignment that boxing was making her sick.

"Killer's beginning to slow down. He's dropping his right hand and it won't be long before Wild Man zeroes in for the kill."

"And then what?" She shuddered as Flanagan's trainer poured a bucket of water over the fighter's head.

Stanley looked at her and shrugged. "Then he wins and we all go off to the victory party."

"Like I said before, count me out."

The bell sounded. Flanagan leaped to his feet and met Killer Curtis in the center of the ring.

"You're right," she said to Stanley Moses. "Curtis is dropping his right hand. He might as well shine a spotlight on his jaw because—"

It was all over.

In the blink of an eye, Wild Man reared back and delivered a powerful wallop to Killer's unprotected face, which sent the other man crashing to the canvas. The referee squatted down by Curtis while Wild Man paced back and forth a few feet away.

"One...two...three..." The referee's voice boomed from the arena's sound system.

Flynn couldn't tear her eyes away from Flanagan's muscled back. There was nothing hidden about his power, nothing subtle.

"...four...five..."

Flanagan was coiled tight. She imagined she could feel his tension, feel the rage and anger that fueled a man like that.

"...six...seven..."

Lenny "Killer" Curtis made a desultory attempt at standing upright but apparently thought better of it and slumped back to the canvas. Smart man. Who on earth would willingly face another round of punishment?

"...eight...nine..."

The crowd was on its feet, screaming for Wild Man Flanagan. Television crews pressed up against the ropes, blocking her view. Flynn kicked off her shoes and climbed upon her seat once again, craning her neck for a glimpse of the champion.

Flanagan had stopped pacing and stood at Killer Curtis's feet. *He cares,* Flynn thought, watching his face. It was more than the money and the bright lights; Flanagan actually cared about his opponent. Another fighter would have claimed victory like a lion claiming his pride. Few people in this world gave a damn about anything more than the almighty buck, and it stunned Flynn to encounter real concern in such an unlikely place.

You'd expect concern like that in a hospital or—

A hospital room. A dark-haired boy with fierce eyes and gentle hands.

Strange. She hadn't thought about the hospital for ages. Certainly not in detail. Now twice in one evening she had felt herself being pulled back into the past. Why on earth would she think about that awful time now? Or about the boy who had rescued her?

Great sports reporter she'd make. Perhaps it was a good thing she made her living with her face and not her intellect, after all. *Get with it, Mary,* she ordered herself. *Worry about today.*

"...ten!" The referee grabbed Flanagan's right arm and held it aloft, and the arena rocked with cheers.

She tapped a cheering Stanley Moses on the shoulder. "Wild Man won?"

"Real sports animal, aren't you, Flynn?" Stanley shook his head in dismay. "You better believe he won. Knockout."

She looked back at the ring, at the undefeated champion. "He doesn't look very happy."

"You wouldn't look too happy either, if you'd spent five rounds getting hell beaten out of you."

"It's more than that," she said, her words lost in the happy chaos all around her. Flanagan broke away from the referee and extended a hand to his opponent. Curtis got to his feet and the two men embraced in the quick, embarrassed way of American males.

I'll take care of you ... I'll never let anything happen ...

"Flynn?"

She blinked and found herself leaning her full weight against Stanley's less-than-mighty shoulder. "I'm fine." She climbed back down from her seat and slipped into her shoes once again. "I felt a little dizzy."

"The heat?"

Her gaze found Flanagan. "Yes."

Flanagan towered over the scores of photographers and reporters crowded into the ring with him. A reporter in the row behind Flynn bellowed out his congratulations, and Flanagan turned in their direction.

His bruised cheekbone was the color of eggplant. A trickle of blood oozed from a cut beneath his right eye. His gaze traveled quickly as he searched for the reporter, sliding from face to face to—

His smile was pagan. Wicked. Entirely too sensual for his own good. And that smile was directed straight at Flynn.

He said something to a man next to him then turned back to the television cameras. She wondered how he would look in someone's living room, all civilized and dressed in a suit and tie, making polite conversation with a stockbroker. She couldn't bring the image to life.

He wasn't like anyone she knew. He was probably semiliterate with a vocabulary limited to "yes," "no," and "hey, baby." Flynn was sure his women were limited to the bedroom and the kitchen, bleached blondes whose single-digit IQs matched his. He was thirty years old and at the end of his career, and any adult in his or her right mind would feel nothing but pity for him—at least, anyone foolish enough to care.

She followed Stanley out of the arena, elbowing her way past rich sycophants and blue-collar New Yorkers who'd hocked their Chevys to buy a ticket to Paradise Island to see the fight of the century. Limos, jitney buses and taxis clogged the street in front of the arena.

Stanley flagged down a cab and held the door for Flynn.

"I'll drop you off at the hotel," he said to her as the driver angled the battered cab in front of a white Rolls.

"Don't go out of your way, Stanley."

"No problem. We pass the Hilton on the way to the party."

The driver swiveled around and looked at them. "I have a good shortcut, man. Get you to your party in no time."

Stanley shook his head. "Gotta take the lady back to the Hilton."

"No, you don't," said Flynn. "Take the short-cut."

Stanley stared at her. "The party?"

She stared right back at him. "The party."

He threw back his head and laughed. "Making sure you earn your paycheck?"

Flynn flashed him her best $2000-per-day smile. "You could say that."

You could also say that nothing on earth could have kept her away from seeing Wild Man Flanagan again.

UNFORTUNATELY THE PARTY did not live up to expectations. Flynn had been there for over two hours and Wild Man Flanagan had yet to make an appearance. No one had expected him to pull a pair of jeans over his boxing trunks and zoom right over to the hotel ballroom, but it seemed to Flynn as if he should have put in an appearance by now, if only to take his bows.

The smell of victory—of power—was in the air.

Men in expensive silk suits fell over their Gucci shoes in an attempt to find the glamorous warrior. They jostled one another for the chance to shake hands with raw strength.

Few people in life were lucky enough to be cheered simply for doing a day's work. Most of them would never miss an opportunity. Wild Man, it would appear, was not your average man. She wondered if he'd been hurt more seriously than his huge smile after the fight might indicate. Or, worse yet, had he picked out a handful of placard-toting nymphets and repaired to the nearest hot tub?

She wasn't jealous. No, it was nothing like that. She didn't care what he did—or with whom.

But still . . .

She was drawn to him in a way she couldn't explain or understand, almost as if some force outside herself was urging her on.

And it wasn't as if she was asking much of the encounter.

She just wanted to see him up close. Hear the sound of his voice. Know how it felt to stand next to raw male power. That's all she wanted; as soon as she'd accomplished her goal, she'd turn around and head home and she wouldn't ask for more.

"GREAT FIGHT, WILD MAN." Donald Trump grinned and shook Jack's hand.

"Hope you made a few bucks on it," said Jack.

The billionaire flashed Jack a thumbs-up sign. "We'll be talking. I have a few ideas that might interest you."

Jack nodded and sipped his champagne, wincing as the liquid stung the inside of his mouth. Damn, but he'd taken a few good shots from Lenny. His face was bruised already, and he'd be sporting a shiner come morning. Hell of a way to make a living.

"How you doin'?" Oscar popped up at his right elbow with a plate of caviar, toast points, and a thick slab of cheese.

"Hungry," said Jack, filching a piece of the cheese. He'd never acquired a taste for the foods rich people found so irresistible. "I thought we ordered some real food for this bash."

Oscar, who had had no trouble adjusting to the so-called finer things in life, pointed toward a buffet table in the rear of the ballroom. "Red meat, cholesterol and preservatives are back there. Help yourself."

Jack grinned and polished off the rest of his champagne. "Do they have Coors over there, too?"

Oscar groaned. "Damn it, kid! When you gonna learn about class?"

"Probably never." He gestured toward the custom-made tux he wore. "This is the last time you'll see me in a getup like this."

Oscar gave him an awkward pat on the back. "Your time is just startin', kid. The offers are pouring in. Trump's got a deal pendin' for you, and Hollywood is talking seven figures. You're in demand."

"Yeah," Jack muttered. "Right. Every billionaire needs himself a pet prizefighter."

Oscar's fuzzy gray brows knitted. "Lenny rattled your brains that bad?"

"Bad enough. Let's just say I'm getting out at the right time."

Oscar touched his forearm. "You want me to make you an appointment with Dr. Salvini?"

Jack shook his head. "My ego's what hurts the most, Oscar. I should've taken him out in the first round."

He was right, and Oscar was too honest a man to argue with Jack. The men fell silent as two elegant blondes drifted past them, cool and enticing in strapless black dresses.

"Why do you want to mess with that red meat and jazz?" Oscar asked, his eyes following the women's progress through the room. "Those gals are headin' for the fish eggs or my name ain't Oscar Davis. That's where the smart money spends their time."

The blondes were beautiful. No doubt about it. They were probably available, too. They had that brittle sexiness Jack had learned was as fake as their hair color.

"Forget it," said Jack, turning away from them. "I need some food."

It took a half hour to make his way across the massive ballroom. Guests, at varying levels of drunkenness, stopped him every few feet to slap him on the back, kiss his cheek, pick his pockets, and stroke his ego. A muscle in his jaw started twitching halfway across the room, and he found himself struggling to remain polite and civilized.

Usually after a fight he was loose and easy; adrenaline pumping at a fever pitch but the anger inside him gone. Tonight was different. The adrenaline still flowed, but the anger remained, and with it, a healthy dose of fear. He was thirty years old and at the end of the line. His career was over. No more bright lights. No more climbing into the ring, primed and ready to fight. No wife waiting for him to come home. No kids. He had nothing to show for the past ten years except a prison record and a big bank account.

Maybe he should double back and head for the caviar-and-champagne blondes. Maybe he should suggest a walk on the beach and a trip to—

And then he saw her in the doorway. A tall, slender woman in a dress of midnight blue. A woman with a fall of wavy auburn hair that danced around her delicate face and narrow shoulders like living fire. She wore high-heeled sandals and a thin silver chain around her waist, and the supple blue dress left little to his imagination. Her hips were rounded, her belly flat. Her breasts were high and full; her nipples were hard and visible against the soft fabric of her dress. He imagined them, taut and demanding, against the heated flesh of his palm.

She glided into the room as if she owned the place. She wasn't the kind of woman who could slip through a crowd unnoticed, and he watched, eyes narrowed, as she greeted men and women alike with a kiss on the cheek and a quick, sure smile. She had the elegant thoroughbred limbs of a model. With each step she took, her short skirt flashed him a glimpse of her slender thighs.

He wanted her.

He forgot about food and started toward her, unmindful of the commotion he caused as he brushed past old friends and new in his eagerness to meet the red-haired woman. A tall man with a blond mustache tapped her on the shoulder then swept her up into a bear hug. Jack's fists clenched at his side. It had been eight years since he'd wanted to belt somebody outside of the ring; right now he wanted to pick that man up off his feet and slam him into the wall.

Real civilized, Flanagan. You've come a long way. Getting a little possessive about somebody you don't even know, aren't you?

She gracefully untangled herself from the blond man's hold and veered toward the hallway once again. He doubled back, waylaid for a moment by a cameraman who effectively tangled Jack in a maze of cord and wire. By the time he disentangled himself, the girl was halfway out the door.

He'd worry about the questions later. He shoved his way through a cluster of Fortune 500 widows as he wondered how it would feel to die in her arms.

BY THE END OF THE THIRD HOUR, Flynn had had enough. The atmosphere in the ballroom was as smoky and noisy as the atmosphere in the sports arena had been, and she wanted nothing more than to get out.

"What about meeting the champ?" Stanley asked as she said her goodbyes. "I owe you an intro."

She kissed Stanley's cheek. "You don't owe me anything. I owe *you* a story."

"Semantics," he said with a wave of his hand.

"I'll see you back in New York." She turned and headed for the door.

The melancholy feeling that had descended upon Flynn during the fight still lingered. She didn't know if it was the champagne or the heat, but she felt as if she were walking through heavy fog as she smiled and nodded her way toward the exit. *At least admit it to yourself,* she thought. *The only reason you came to this stupid party was to meet Wild Man Flanagan.*

"Stupid," she said out loud as she reached the door. "Childish, stupid and—"

"Wait."

She stopped cold. The man's voice was dark, husky and extraordinarily commanding, and she knew beyond doubt that he was talking to her. *Get out,* a voice warned. *Get out while there's still time.* She pushed open the door; a large male hand pulled it closed.

A fluttering sensation sprang to life in her belly as she drew in a deep, shaky breath. "Look," she said,

"I don't know what the game is but—" She turned and found herself face-to-face with Wild Man Flanagan.

There was little to remind her of the incredible machine she had watched in the ring a few hours earlier. Although he was built on a larger-than-life scale, the only signs of Wild Man were the bruises on his cheekbone and the cut near his lip. His eyes were dark blue and infinitely sad, his mouth wide and sensual. The tux barely restrained his powerfully muscular frame.

"I wanted to meet you."

"That's my line," said Flynn, struggling to maintain her composure. Dear God, how could such a violent man have such a seductive voice?

"Johnny Flanagan." Her hand disappeared inside his.

"Flynn."

He grinned, exposing large and surprisingly even white teeth. "Just Flynn?"

His grip was strong and firm, just as she had imagined it would be. "Just Flynn. No one expects a model to be smart enough to remember two names." Her past was her own; she did her best to keep it that way.

"Fight fan?"

She glanced down at her right hand, which was still hidden inside his, then back up at him. There was no laughter in his eyes, no innuendo. What she saw there was as blatant and powerful as the heat building inside her body. For a moment she was nothing but pure sensation.

"Fight fan?" he repeated.

"Afraid not. This was my first."

"Did you like it?"

"No." She laughed self-consciously at her own bluntness. "Violence terrifies me."

"It's a violent world."

"Agreed, but why encourage it?"

Still her hand in his. Still the heat in her belly and breasts. Still the strange feeling of being exactly where she was meant to be.

He took a step closer to her. The side of her right arm brushed against his powerful chest, and a wave of desire, intense and primitive, washed over her.

"Are you always this honest?" he asked.

"No, I'm not." *Flynn, stop! This man is dangerous. He isn't for you....* She met his eyes, willed him to see inside her heart. She made her living fulfilling fantasies, becoming whatever the photographer wanted her to be. How much easier it was to take on the colors of the people around her than to allow anyone to see the scarlet rage and black loneliness inside her soul. "Most of the time I tell people exactly what they want to hear."

He brought his mouth closer to her, so close she caught the smell of tobacco and whiskey on his breath. A man's smell. She could get drunk on the smell of him.

"You won't do that with me," he said, lips brushing the curve of her ear. "I don't want anything less than the truth."

"Yes," she breathed, legs trembling with a force beyond reason, beyond wisdom. She had no choice. He knew her inside and out. "I don't understand this. I feel—"

"I know." He held her hand against his heart, and she felt the wild pounding of his blood. "It's the same for me."

He would overwhelm a woman. Flynn knew without being told that loving him and being loved by him would be an all-consuming passion. There would be no room for rhyme or reason; there would be no halfway measures. He would demand everything from the woman he wanted, heart and soul and body, and wouldn't hesitate to steal the part she tried to call her own.

"You frighten me," she said as the pulsing of her blood matched his.

"I'll never hurt you."

She looked at this man whom she had watched reign supreme over a crowd of thousands with nothing but the power in his two fists, and she believed him. "I trust you," she said softly, "and that frightens me even more."

"Let's get out of here." He urged her toward the exit. "Let's get away from the crowd."

She turned her head slightly and saw the throng of people surging toward them. She saw the questions and the laughter and the envy in their eyes. "It's your party. You should stay here."

"Not now." He put his arm around her waist and propelled her out the door. "It doesn't matter anymore."

Later on many people would say they were there when it happened. They would say it was as obvious as lightning across a summer night's sky and twice as electrifying. But, in truth, it was a small moment—a brief flicker of acknowledgement, of *destiny*, that left both Flynn and Jack shaken to their cores.

The sultry night air was welcoming after the sharp chill of air conditioning inside the ballroom. Jack waved away his driver and led Flynn down a long path that curved toward the beach. The sky was hazy with moisture; the stars seemed blurred, softer than usual. Flynn, however, was sharply aware of the sights and sounds and smells around her. The silvery splash of moonlight against the sand. The eternal rush of the ocean. The sting of salt air mingled with the high, sweet scent of hibiscus and gardenias.

And the intoxicating knowledge that the man she walked with was dangerous in every sense of the word. She was no match for him in strength. She had seen the way he dominated his opponent. If he wanted her, there would be little she could do to stop him from taking her right there on the sand.

She knew that idea should terrify her.

It didn't.

What it did was make her want him in a way so savage, so pagan, that it hurt to breathe.

They walked in silence for a few minutes, tracing a path along the curve of shoreline away from the hotel. Lights from a pleasure boat twinkled in the distance, looking soft and magical against the darkness. She looked up at him, marvelling at the strong, almost cruel, profile and the sharp angle of his jaw. There was nothing yielding about his expression, nothing except the sensual fullness of his lower lip.

She longed to sink her teeth into his lower lip, feel its succulence against her tongue.

She was losing her mind.

The beach curved toward a secluded cove where they stopped walking. The hotel was nothing but a blur of light and sound.

They faced each other. They didn't touch. She looked into those beautiful and sad eyes of his and her heart cracked wide open. There was no place to hide, no place to run.

There was no place else on earth she wanted to be.

JACK KNEW HE HAD COME as close to heaven as a sinner ever managed when he looked into her eyes. He had forgotten beauty such as hers could exist in such an ugly world. It had been years since he'd been so deeply, powerfully, moved by the sight and smell of a woman. The last time had been ten years ago when he fell in love with Mary. Delicate, beautiful Mary with her—

Maybe he had been punched one time too many. Why in hell was he thinking about that long ago bride when a woman of flesh and blood was a breath away? Flynn was nothing like Mary. Mary had been young and fragile and silvery-blond. Flynn was older, sexier, with fiery red hair and thrusting breasts.

Only the look in her eyes was the same: an open, honest look of such emptiness and longing that he wondered what it would take to erase that look forever.

Dangerous, Flanagan. This woman is more dangerous than anyone you've met in the ring. He knew how to deal with men. You told them exactly what you think, and if that didn't work, you let your fists do the talking for you. It had worked when he was twenty and it worked now, albeit with a difference. When he was twenty, he went to jail for talking with his fists.

Now, at thirty, he got paid for it.

He reached out and touched her cheek. Her skin was soft, warm, infinitely female. Gently he traced the proud curve of her cheekbone, the strong angle of her jaw, the silky length of her throat. She watched him through half-closed lids, those blue eyes of hers looking deep into his soul.

He drew his finger along the outline of her collarbone and smiled when she gasped softly as his hand slid over the upper curve of her breast.

He wasn't a subtle man but he was a fair one. "I want you," he said, meeting her gaze.

"I know." Her voice was a whisper against the rush of the ocean.

"I don't take women against their will."

She said nothing, just watched him. Those eyes...

He forced himself to step away from her warmth, to give her the chance to leave if that was what she wanted. She stood there, arms at her sides, and didn't move.

He felt sixteen again, all emotions and hormones, as frightened and nervous as he'd been the very first time. His pulse hammered in his ears and made it hard to think.

"Say something, Flynn." His voice was rough with desire. "Tell me what you want."

She said nothing, but in that instant when he teetered at the edge of despair, she raised her arms wide to him, and he stepped forward to stake his claim.

Chapter Seven

Flynn had never felt more vulnerable—or more womanly—in her life. The simple act of opening her arms to him was the most dangerous thing she had ever done. But there was no hope for it; from the first moment she looked into his eyes, she knew where they would end up.

She was tall, but still he towered over her. She rested her head against his broad chest and gloried in the strong, steady beat of his heart beneath her ear. There was something magnificent, almost pagan, in the sensation of being overwhelmed by the sheer size of a man. He held her full against him, and she feared she would never catch her breath.

His hands slid over her back to her rib cage, his large fingers spanning the distance from waist to breast. With each breath she managed to take, the lower curve of her breasts brushed against his hand, and she took intense pleasure in his obvious response. She moved slightly away and slid her hands between them, moving up his chest. His jacket dropped to the sand, and he ripped open his shirt. The buttons glistened like pearls as they drifted down. She had already seen his body; she knew the masculine beauty of it. Yet, here on the lonely beach, he seemed almost godlike.

Trembling, she moved her hands to his chest, placing her palms flat against him. His skin was hot beneath her fingers; his muscles as hard and smooth as marble. She moved her hands in small circles, delighting in the way his nipples grew hard at her command.

Her breasts ached with longing for his answering touch. Maddeningly he denied her that pleasure and instead moved his hands slowly over her rib cage. She swayed with desire as he toyed with the silver belt slung low over her hips, his fingers sliding between cold metal and pliant flesh.

A heaviness began in her belly as he inched her skirt up higher and higher until her thighs quivered beneath his touch. She was only slightly aware of the quick, supple motion that unhooked her belt.

"Are you sure?" His voice was darker than the night.

She nodded, not trusting her voice.

"Tell me," he urged, thumbs toying with the lace-trimmed edge of her panties. "Tell me what you want."

"I—" She swallowed. Fire coiled its way through her body, searing her mind, burning away logic. She tilted her head back and looked up at him. "I want you to kiss me."

He bent low over her body and brought his mouth to hers. He allowed her no quarter, using tongue and lips and teeth in a sensual assault designed to render her helpless, and he didn't break the kiss until she sagged against him in surrender.

"Now tell me what you want."

"You," she said, unable to disguise the fire in her blood. "I want you."

He swept her into his arms. She felt the tense coil of muscle in his biceps and along his shoulders, and she couldn't resist the urge to draw her tongue lightly over the hollows those muscles created. His body shuddered beneath her touch, and she understood that even a man as powerful as he was helpless before desire. Quickly he crossed the sand and headed toward a small cove a few hundred feet away.

He put her down, and she stood, shivering with both fear and desire, as he drew her flimsy dress up over her breasts and shoulders then tossed it aside. The silver chain already lay coiled like a snake at her feet. Flynn wasn't a fool when it came to the power of her beauty; after all, she made her living because of it. She had used her looks to charm her way out of difficulties, to construct barriers between herself and others, but she had never before used it to bring pleasure to a man. Not like this.

His eyes devoured her. There was nothing subtle about the way his gaze swept over her body from her delicate toes to her knees, to the center of her femininity, up over belly and breasts only to rest finally on her face. She waited for the obligatory "You're beautiful," for Flanagan to reach out to touch her breasts or pull her close to him.

He did none of those. He watched her until her trembling stopped and her fear vanished and only hunger remained. And then when she felt she would die without his touch, he dropped to his knees on the sand and buried his face against the tender flesh at the top of her thighs. His breath was hot and moist. At the first touch of his mouth against her, the air rushed from her lungs and she clung to his shoulders. The earth was spinning wildly on its axis; this man was her only safety.

His huge hands grasped her by the back of her thighs, fingers pressing into the soft inner flesh, urging her on. Still clinging to his shoulders for support, Flynn moaned as he found her with his mouth. Her head fell back and her nails dug more deeply into his muscular shoulders.

Moments—years—later, she sagged against him, spent but not yet sated.

And he knew.

He rose slowly, branding her with his lips and tongue along her rib cage and breasts and throat. She cradled his face between her hands. His mouth glided across her lips, as fiery and as sweet as she had imagined.

"Jack," she murmured, out of her head with fever. Primitive, wordless pleasure coursed through her body. "Oh, please..."

He tilted his head back a fraction to look at her. "Jack," he said, twisting the name as if it were foreign to him. "Nobody's called me Jack for years."

She struggled to regain control of her mind. "It *is* your name, isn't it?" Surely she'd seen it on the card at the fight or heard Stanley call him that.

"I don't remember." He kissed her deeply. "This isn't the place, Flynn. Will you come home with me?"

He could be a madman or a genius, a sinner or a saint. It didn't matter. Flynn said yes.

He slipped into his shirt and jacket. "Lift your arms."

She did as he asked, like an obedient child, and her silky dress slithered over her body. He clasped the belt about her waist again, hands lingering at her waist. She was in thrall to him completely, a slave to the oldest lure of all.

"My shoes," she said, looking around the sand for them.

He patted the right pocket of his jacket. "All taken care of."

Her face blazed with heat. "And my panties?"

The look on his face was darkly sensual, exquisitely dangerous. "I have them."

Her eyes closed for a moment as a wave of incendiary heat threatened what remained of her sanity. This was uncharted territory, the dark and dangerous waters of sexuality that most people never ventured into. *It's not too late,* an inner voice warned. *You can still say no.*

But, of course, she didn't. The same force—dark and dangerous and infinitely compelling—that had driven her to meet him was still at work. She had believed it would be enough to meet him, to hear his voice. But it hadn't been. Not even the touch of his hand or his lips against her had been enough to quench the primitive desire within.

And yet this was beyond desire. Beyond reason. Beyond anything she had known before—or anything she had ever imagined. She wanted him to take her, to overpower her with his strength, to cradle her close to his chest and make her feel safe and secure. He was danger and solace. He was a walk on the wild side, yet no one had ever made her feel more protected.

He took her hand and led her up the beach to where his car and driver waited. He waved for the driver to remain behind the wheel and helped Flynn into the limo. She was painfully conscious of the way her skirt rode up her thighs and of the fact that her lacy bikini panties were tucked away in one of his pockets.

Flanagan said something to his driver before climbing in, and Flynn breathed a sigh of relief when the dark glass privacy shield whirred softly up, shielding her from curious eyes.

As it turned out, there was nothing for anyone, curious or not, to see or hear. She and Flanagan rode in silence. Their thighs brushed once as the driver took a sharp turn, and Flynn's entire body registered the heat from his body. She felt dizzy, drunk almost, with desire. Her blood flowed thick and heavy in her veins; she could still feel the devastating thrill of his mouth against her, his tongue—

The car slid to a stop in front of a luxury hotel on the other side of the island. Flanagan was out in a flash, and the next instant he opened her door and she stepped out of the comforting darkness of the limousine, into a brightly lit courtyard. Still no overt display of affection from Flanagan, save for taking her hand as they walked up the pathway. As if from a distance, she heard the click-click of a camera. Flanagan turned toward the sound, but they only saw a middle-aged man and woman in Bermuda shorts kissing behind a bougainvillea.

Flanagan acknowledged the desk clerk with a nod and strode with Flynn toward the private elevator at the other end of the lobby.

"Everyone must think you're still at the party," Flynn said as they entered the lift.

He said nothing. Her heartbeat accelerated.

"It was a wonderful party," she continued, toying with the clasp of her silver chain belt. "The ice sculpture was one of the best I've seen." *You don't even like ice sculptures, Mary Flynn.* She forced a sheepish grin. "I'm babbling."

"You're scared."

"No, I'm not."

"Yeah?" He dragged a hand through his thick mane of curly dark hair. "I am."

Her laugh was unforced. "Nice try, but I don't buy it."

He met her eyes. "I'm not kidding. You scare the hell out of me, lady."

She playfully made a muscle. "I don't think I'm a threat."

"There've been a lot of women," he said, not returning her smile, "but no one has ever made me feel this way before."

"You don't have to sweet-talk me," she said. "I'm not going to change my mind."

He stepped closer. "Don't give me credit for being a nice guy, Flynn. We've gone too far now to stop."

He stepped closer. She swallowed hard.

"It's still a free country, Flanagan."

He cupped her chin in one massive hand. "It never was. Everything has its price."

"Not this."

"Especially this." He pulled her close and kissed her breathless.

The doors slid open at the penthouse floor, and an instant later Flynn was alone with a man she'd known for less than three hours, yet trusted completely. None of it made sense, yet it seemed as right to her as breathing.

"A drink?"

She shook her head. She was already out of control. He dimmed the lights a fraction, and she was vaguely aware of a great deal of chrome and glass and thick, lush carpeting. But she was more aware of Flanagan. He'd draped his jacket over the back of the couch and his shirt hung open, exposing his magnificent chest. Her mouth went dry at the sight of him moving toward her. He was a pirate king, a dark angel, every midnight fantasy she'd ever had, come to blazing life before her.

He took her hand and placed it over his heart.

"See?" He kissed her palm. "You scare me, Flynn."

She met his eyes. "I'm no match for you," she said, her voice soft. "Not in any way I can think of."

The look he gave her made her heart thud painfully against her rib cage. "In every way." His expression was unguarded, and in his eyes she saw a vulnerability that touched something inside her soul.

"I'm glad."

He placed her hand flat against his erection and her breath caught audibly.

"So am I," he said.

She'd been aware of her sexual power for a very long while; this was the first time she'd ever used it away from the camera.

"Flanagan?"

He met her gaze.

"Take your shirt off for me."

He didn't smile; he didn't say a word. His eyes darkened as he slid first his right arm and then his left from the sleeves and tossed the shirt onto the floor.

"My God, you're beautiful." She hadn't meant to say those words. She didn't even realize she had uttered them until she saw the red stains on his cheeks. He was built on a grand—and intimidating—scale. For the first time in her life she understood why ancient cultures had worshiped masculine perfection. She simply had never seen it before that moment.

His chest was smooth, hot to the touch. She brushed her lips against the line of his collarbone, making his heat and scent her own. His hands caressed her hair, stroked her back, then in one elegant motion he swept her up into his arms as if she were a child.

"I'm going to make love to you," he said as he carried her to the bed.

"I know," she whispered, her head resting against his shoulder.

"Our lives may never be the same."

"I know that, too."

For the second time that night she was naked before him. She felt no shame in nudity and no false modesty about her looks, but there, in front of Flanagan, she had finally met her match. He looked at her body, but he also saw through to her heart and that changed everything.

He ran his hands lightly along her hips, up over the curve of her waist, coming to rest just under her breasts. Teasing. Caressing. Promising but never quite delivering the ultimate fulfillment.

He laid Flynn down atop the huge bed and looked at her for the longest moment of her life. Nothing escaped his dark gaze. He asked her a necessary question, and she answered honestly. She was pleased he cared enough to do the right thing for them both.

And then he was on the mattress next to her. Those long, powerful limbs of his covering hers. That muscular chest pressed against her breasts. The hands clutching her buttocks, kneading her firm flesh with masterful strokes that made her whimper with need. She had never wanted a man the way she wanted Flanagan, never wanted a man in quite the same way or with the same ferocious intensity. There wasn't a part of her body that didn't crave his touch. There wasn't a part of her body that didn't ache to be filled by him.

The full-bodied smell of sexuality blossomed around them, and they touched each other with the assurance of long-time lovers even as the excitement of discovery made their blood pulse wildly through their veins. How could something so new, so dangerous, feel so natural? So right?

His moan was low and deep as he entered her, then he rolled over onto his back, taking her with him. Her knees were on either side of his hips and he held her firmly by the waist.

"Jack..." she breathed as he filled her past reason.

"Open your eyes. I've waited a long time for this, Flynn."

Such an odd thing to say. Still, she understood. They'd known each other only hours and yet it seemed to Flynn as if this night, this moment, had been ordained from the beginning of time.

JACK HAD BEEN REINING IN his passions for years now. Learning to control his temper. Moderate his anger. Channel his rage and frustration into the ring so more civilized people could pay to watch him beat somebody's brains out all in the name of sport.

Sex had become his safety valve, the one way to relieve the pressure building inside him. He'd quickly learned how to pleasure women, to bring them quickly to climax then take care of his own needs with a minimum of fuss. Never before had he brought his full range of emotions into the bedroom. Never before tonight.

He wanted to crawl inside her mind, curl up inside her heart, worship her body. He wanted to drive himself into her until there were no boundaries between them, until he lost himself in her warmth and sweetness, until the pain he'd carried with him for as long as he could remember was washed away.

Her head was thrown back, the fiery red hair ablaze around her lovely face. He touched the spot where they were joined and was rewarded with a low moan uttered deep in her throat. It was all he could do to keep from exploding within her.

But it was too soon for that.

He reached up and cupped her full breasts, savoring their soft roundness against his calloused hands.

He couldn't remember encountering softness such as that before. The feel was almost enough to drive him over the edge into madness. *Take it easy with her,* a voice warned. There were times when he forgot his own power, frightening people with his intensity and strength. He didn't want to scare her. She was so beautiful and womanly and—

"Don't hold back," she said against his mouth. "Don't hold back with me."

He hesitated a second—did she understand all her words implied?—then madness ruled. He rolled over with her, covered her. Then he drove into her, filling her, moving in and out with a desperate, yearning rhythm that transcended space and time.

"You're mine," he said in that split second before he shattered and died. "You'll always be mine."

Her cry of pleasure was the only answer he needed.

"Honey, wake up."

In New York City Ryder O'Neal groaned and tried to ignore his wife's voice in his ear.

"Ryder!" That elbow in the ribs he couldn't ignore. "It's your turn."

He pulled the pillow over his face. "How come it's always my turn at six in the morning?"

Joanna's chuckle sounded altogether too cheerful, considering the hour. "Ask your daughter that."

"I think it's a conspiracy."

She rolled closer and pressed a warm kiss against his shoulder. Four years married and her nearness still moved him. He was a lucky man.

But it was still six in the morning.

"Go get her," Joanna said, stifling a yawn. "I'll do the rest."

He threw back the covers and dragged his poor, tired, just-shy-of-forty body from the bed. "You better do the rest." He didn't even try to stifle his yawn. "You're breast-feeding."

"Wait until we have a second one. We'll have wall-to-wall diapers."

"No second one," Ryder muttered as he stumbled into Kerry's nursery. "This kid's going to be an only child."

A likely story, he thought as he looked down at his first miracle. Kerry bestowed the toothless smile of an eight-month-old upon him and his heart melted. He bent over the crib and scooped up his little girl into his arms. She blinked her eyes comically and one chubby fist grabbed at the hair on his chest.

"Ouch!" he said, wincing as she gave a tug. "That's real."

The baby gurgled with delight and tugged again.

"Wait until you have three or four little brothers and sisters around here to contend with," he warned, pressing a kiss against her pudgy hand. "We'll see how good a big sister you are, Kerry Lynn O'Neal."

Of course, she'd be absolutely perfect. Ryder hadn't the slightest doubt. Having Kerry was the best thing they'd ever done—and probably the most unexpected. Children had never been high up on his list of things to do. While he'd envied his brothers their contentment, he had never envied them their children.

Children tied you down.

Children changed your life.

Children forced you to think about the future when you'd rather think about today.

All of the clichés were one hundred percent true. But what nobody mentioned was the amazing transformation of your heart the first time you held that incredible bundle of hopes and dreams.

How badly he'd underestimated the power of love.

Kerry started to fuss. "Okay, little one," he said, heading back toward the master bedroom. "Mom is all ready and—"

Asleep.

Joanna was sitting up in bed, sound asleep. Her shiny black hair fell across her face like an ebony veil and drifted onto her shoulders. She'd been struggling with caring for the baby, the apartment, the minutiae involved in their move from Manhattan to a home in Connecticut, and—in her spare time—working as Holland Chambers's makeup artist on her prime-time TV series.

He looked at his sleeping wife then down at his hungry baby daughter. "Your mom's right," he said moments later in the kitchen as his daughter watched him warm a bottle. "It's time we got out of the city and into a nice big suburban tract house with room for you to run around."

He heard a thud outside the apartment door as the Sunday papers hit the welcome mat. Now that was something he'd miss up there in Connecticut. Few sounds in the world were more satisfying than that of the *New York Times* landing at your front door.

He opened the apartment door and bent down to retrieve the papers.

"Look at this," he said to Kerry who watched his every move. "Someone stuck the *Daily News* in here, too."

Might as well see how the Yankees were doing before he deserted the Bronx Bombers for New England's best.

He never got there. Smeared across the front page, ahead of news on Lebanon, Nicaragua and the budget deficit was the banner headline: Wild Man Goes Out Swinging, followed by the heavyweight champ's impressive statistics. But it wasn't the report of the fight that caught Ryder's attention; it was the photograph that accompanied it.

Like everyone else, Ryder had seen Flanagan's face a thousand times before, plastered on sports pages from New York to L.A. and all points in between. And Flynn's gorgeous face wasn't exactly unknown in the western hemisphere. He was always glad to see Mary Flynn Scott looking happy and beautiful. She deserved it.

They were two perfect physical specimens. The photographer had caught them entering a small, exclusive hotel on Paradise Island and even in a grainy, one-dimensional newspaper photo, the heat between them was almost palpable.

It wasn't hard to remember when things were different for both of them.

RYDER HAD STORMED OUT of Alistair Chambers's apartment that hot July afternoon ten years ago and headed across town toward the hospital. Chambers had given him his walking papers when it came to

Hugh Scott's detail, but Ryder still had unfinished business.

Mary Flynn was lying in a hospital bed. Billy Pennington, one of the brightest lights on the political scene, was dead and buried, and sweet Mary was now a widow. It didn't make sense. Not any of it. This whole story Scott had been given about burned identification smelled of a cover-up, if you asked Ryder. Not that anybody had. Chambers seemed to think there was nothing unusual. "Accidents happen," he had said in that damned cool British manner of his. "Even in this modern age, foul-ups occur."

Foul-ups, hell, Ryder thought as he jaywalked across Lexington Avenue. If what Chambers had told him was true, Hugh Scott was a member of PAX, the largest and most powerful source of information—both classified and not—in the world. As his only living relative, wouldn't Mary Flynn figure somewhere in the scheme of things? Scott must have known about the wedding. Hell, Ryder knew all about the wedding and he wasn't family. He'd even wondered why Scott didn't fly back for the small ceremony she'd had planned.

The meeting in Geneva had already wound down, and Ryder doubted if any of the diplomats would have looked askance if Scott had zipped back to the States to stand up for his only niece.

"He's a man of honor." Chambers's words ate at Ryder's gut. "He had a job to do and he did it. You, my boy, should understand that."

Ryder did. He knew all about personal sacrifice and doing what the organization told you to do, your own happiness be damned. But that didn't change a thing.

Scott claimed his niece had eloped but Ryder didn't buy it.

Disaster seemed to follow Mary Flynn. First her father died suddenly, then two members of her father's cabinet, one of whom was William Pennington, Sr., her husband's father and Secretary of State.

Not her husband, he thought, swearing softly. Her late husband.

The Scott curse, as it had come to be known, was alive and well and it had zeroed in on Mary Flynn again.

Ryder had to see Scott once more before Chambers had him assigned to a fishing trawler off the coast of Alaska. He had to see Mary Flynn and offer her his sympathy and support. But more importantly, he had to see Scott and Mary together. Watch how Scott played the doting and devoted uncle of America's brave little girl.

And if he still had this gnawing in his gut, he'd storm right back to Chambers's apartment, knock down the door and force the pigheaded Englishman to put aside logic for once and take a chance on intuition.

At the hospital Ryder flashed a government service card, a handy-dandy PAX item, and took the elevator up to the fourth floor. It didn't take more than a second to see all hell had broken loose up there. He patted his pocket, checking for his service revolver, and headed toward what was left of the nurses' station.

A hole had been bashed into the front of the counter. Papers, folders and X rays were scattered from one end of the floor to the other. Broken cups, glasses and thousands of brightly colored pills and capsules littered the desk and countertops. The floor-to-ceiling cabinets that once lined the walls were upside down in the corner of the room.

An exhausted-looking gray-haired nurse manned the desk.

"Border skirmish?" Ryder asked as she looked up.

The nurse's mouth tilted downward. "If you're from the police, he's down there." She gestured toward the narrow hallway with the eraser end of her pencil, then looked back at her work, almost as if she wasn't sitting in the midst of total chaos.

"I'm looking for Mary Scott."

She didn't look up. "Who?"

"Mary Scott. Car accident. Young."

"The girl in 402." She glanced up for a second. "You're too late. She's gone."

Ryder's knees buckled. "Not Mary..."

"Oh, she's not dead," said the nurse, touching his hand. "She's gone home."

"What?"

"Her uncle came and took her an hour ago."

"Didn't waste any time, did he?"

"Sir?"

"Nothing. Do you know where they went?"

"I couldn't find that information if I wanted to."

Ryder made to leave then turned back. "Who did this?" He motioned toward the mess all around them.

The nurse sighed and removed her eyeglasses, rubbing at her temples with the pads of her thumbs. "Bad business. I told the boy he was getting in too deep."

"This had something to do with Mary?"

Her eyes were lined, but sharp and uncompromising. "They were falling in love."

"You've got to be kidding." Mary was a newly-wed, a bride.

"He saved her, you know. Found her in the burning car. Got himself some pretty nasty burns in the process."

That explained it. "She was grateful," said Ryder. "She owes him her life."

"It's more than that. The boy guarded her like she was a princess in a castle. There were times I didn't know if he'd let us near her. When her uncle showed up, he—" She shook her head and Ryder saw tears glistening in her tired eyes. "Well, it's over now. She's gone, and the police are on their way for him. A real shame. The boy has a heart. If only he could have controlled that temper."

Ryder thanked her and headed toward the elevator banks. There was no point talking to the boy. The boy didn't know anything about Mary Scott. All he knew was a girl in need, a girl without any past at all. He pressed the down button and waited. Why in hell had he come to the hospital? He had no idea what he would have said to Mary, had she still been there. There was no reason in the world she'd remember him from a diplomatic party three years earlier. Ryder was just one of many faceless, nameless operatives moving in the shadows. He'd been a fool to think his concern mattered. Hugh Scott was an entity unto himself, and he had his niece's welfare in hand.

Maybe Alistair had been right when he said Ryder's personal feelings were getting in the way of his professional duties. Just because he hated Hugh

Scott's guts was no reason to believe he'd done anything against his country—or his late brother, for that matter. Ryder had a notoriously short fuse and this might be one of those occasions when that short fuse got him in trouble.

The elevator doors slid open in front of him, and just as Ryder was about to step inside, he heard a crash from down the hall, followed by the cry of a soul in pain.

He headed toward the noise. The gray-haired nurse didn't look up as he ran by. A cop stood at the end of the hallway and barred Ryder from going any farther. Not even the PAX-designed ID card did any good.

"Mr. Scott's orders," said the cop as a tall kid with huge shoulders was dragged from the room in cuffs.

Ryder pressed back against the wall as the kid passed. The boy's eyes were wild with fear and grief. Blood ran from a cut under his eye, and it wasn't hard to tell his shoulder had been dislocated in a scuffle. He was muscular without being bulky, the kind of big, good-looking Irish kid who thirty years ago would have been dragged off to a gym where he could take out his aggressions on a speedbag instead of being hustled off to jail.

"Just lemme see her," the kid said as they dragged him past Ryder. "You gotta let me see her just once."

"We don't gotta do anything," said the cop on his right. "Now shut up before you get in more trouble, Flanagan."

Ryder watched as they hustled the kid into another room for questioning. He grabbed a detective who was chatting up a student nurse.

"That kid—Flanagan. I want to pay the damages."

The detective tore himself away from the jailbait blonde. "Who are you?"

For the third time Ryder flashed his ID. "That kid saved the girl's life. He deserves better than this."

"You won't get any argument from me."

"Then tell me what precinct they're taking him to, and I'll go over and take care of things before he gets there."

"Not that easy, pal. He's made himself one powerful enemy. They intend to throw the book at the kid."

"Who does?" Ryder asked, although there was little doubt in his mind.

The detective lowered his voice. "Hugh Scott. He's some big shot in government. For some reason he's got it in for the kid."

"Doesn't make sense, does it?" asked Ryder. "Flanagan saved his niece's life."

"Tell it to the judge," said the detective. "I saw Scott with his niece, and if you ask me, he's got ice water in his veins." The detective shook his head sadly. "They had to sedate her to get her out of here."

It was nearly dusk when Ryder left the hospital. Chambers had been right to yank him from the Scott retinue. Hugh Scott was a cold-hearted SOB, and there was nothing Ryder or anyone else could do to change that fact.

As Alistair had pointed out on the telephone, the world needed coldhearted SOBs in order to get anything accomplished. It was the icemen who cut through the emotion and got down to business. The hotter types like Ryder were always getting carried away with intuition and anger and, on occasion, love.

He walked as far as Lex and 75th Street. He was tired and jet-lagged and hungry, and he owed Chambers an apology. Why not make that apology over a sirloin at the club?

He stepped into the street to hail a cab as the light changed. A cop's car pulled up in the right-hand lane, and Ryder found himself looking into the eyes of the boy who'd trashed the nurses' station. The boy's dark hair was shaggy and long. He probably didn't have enough money to afford a haircut. His features were strong, almost fierce; but it was his eyes that commanded attention. Angry eyes, but haunted. Ryder wasn't given to imagery, but it seemed to him he saw a thousand ghosts warring inside the kid. The kid was young and tough and he was also as scared as hell. He'd done a stupid thing at the hospital, but he'd also saved Mary Flynn's life. That should be worth something.

The light changed to green, and the cop's car sped away. The look in the boy's eyes stayed with Ryder for a long time.

HIS DAUGHTER'S CRYING brought Ryder back to the present. He retrieved her bottle and gave it back to her, his mind scattered. He took a slug of OJ and stared at the photo in the paper for the thousandth time.

"No doubt about it," he muttered. That was the same guy he'd seen that day in the hospital. The same guy who had saved Flynn's life.

Two lost and lonely souls found each other again across the years. They were beautiful and rich and young enough to enjoy it all. The whole story was the stuff Technicolor dreams were made of.

Why then did he have the feeling something terrible was up ahead?

And why was he so sure Hugh Scott was behind it?

Chapter Eight

Flynn was deep in a dream. She was warm and safe, surrounded by love. It had been years since she'd been this happy or felt this hopeful. She hugged her pillow more tightly and squeezed her eyes shut, trying to hold on to this sense of security that she knew would vanish with the coming of daylight.

The sunshine streaming through the window couldn't be denied.

She opened her eyes, and to her surprise, the warm and joyous feeling didn't vanish the way it had after so many other dreams. She *was* warm and safe and surrounded by love, and the reason for this miracle was the man in whose arms she rested.

Flanagan.

His thick head of dark hair was tousled, and she couldn't resist smoothing a curl with the tip of her forefinger. Last night she had cradled his head against her breasts, glorying in the knowledge that she was alive, truly alive, for the first time in years.

She shifted slightly in his arms and rested her cheek against his chest. They had spent the night making love, and her body ached pleasurably from his hands and mouth and body. And yet it hadn't been only sex between them. Something much greater, much more frightening, had happened in the darkness of the night. With their bodies they had said things that Flynn knew neither one of them had the words to express.

The most dangerous man in the world and this was the one who eased Flynn's soul and inflamed her body. What she had done was reckless and crazy. She would have been the first to protest if a friend walked off into the night with a man like Flanagan, yet the rightness of Flynn's decision was inarguable.

You could know a man ten years and not know him as deeply, as intimately, as she knew Flanagan. In that bedroom they had surrendered their former selves completely. There had been no holding back, no hesitation. They had come together with no regrets, and the commitment had been as total as it had been unexpected.

Less than twenty-four hours since they first met and already she couldn't remember life without him at the center of it. "I feel as if I've always known you, Jack," she whispered, "as if you've always been a part of me."

"I have been."

She started at the sound of his voice. "I thought you were asleep."

"No," he said. "I wanted to enjoy every second."

"You must be exhausted."

He grinned and kissed her forehead. "You, too."

She ducked her head, blushing. She hadn't blushed in a very long time. "I meant, after the fight."

"Usually I am. This was out of the ordinary."

She kissed his shoulder. "I'm impressed."

"You should be."

She wriggled out of his grasp and scooted toward the edge of the bed. "I'm going to take a shower." He started to swing his legs out, but she placed a hand against his chest and gently pushed him back down onto the mattress. "Rest. You've earned it."

He grabbed her wrist and pulled her across his torso. "I'm not tired."

She felt him, hard and demanding, against her thigh. "So I've noticed."

"You can shower later."

She shook her head. "I'm dying to wash the spray out of my hair. It's time you saw the real me."

He kissed her then gave her a soft smack on the rump. "Go ahead. I'll call down for breakfast."

You're in for quite a surprise, Flanagan, she thought as she headed for the bathroom.

JACK UNDERSTOOD the differences between the sexes, but it seemed those differences were especially obvious when it came to bathrooms. He ordered them a lavish breakfast from room service, showered in the half-bath next to the second bedroom, and had time to answer three phone calls from an irate Oscar who was threatening to show up on Jack's doorstep for an explanation.

"Where is your brain, man?" Oscar shouted into the phone. "There were reporters crawling all over that place. The second you disappeared, they had you checking into the hospital for brain surgery."

"No brain surgery," said Jack with a short laugh.

"Maybe you could use some," Oscar continued, losing none of his head of steam. "Maybe you got your head punched a time too often. You got responsibilities, kid. You still got a future ahead of you and you—"

Flynn stood in the doorway between bedroom and bath, draped in an oversized white bath towel. The phone fell to the floor as Jack stared at her.

"I know it's a surprise," she said, twisting at a lock of her hair. She laughed nervously. "I *did* tell you I wanted to show you the real me."

He felt as if he were standing in the center of a wind tunnel. Air rushed around him, drowning out thought, as he sank onto the edge of the bed. He was falling backward in time, falling backward toward darkness, toward endless despair.

She walked toward him, and he struggled to hear her words through the haze of memory surrounding him.

"Say something, Jack! I thought most gentlemen preferred blondes."

The fiery red curls were gone. In their place was a cascade of shiny blond hair that fell as straight and true as a waterfall.

It can't be . . . it's not possible . . .

"You must have suspected something," she continued, sitting next to him on the bed. "I mean, my— umm, you know what I'm trying to say."

He knew exactly what she was trying to say. The thick curls at the top of her thighs were a dark gold, but he hadn't thought anything of it one way or the other. Most women played with the color of their hair.

But most women weren't Flynn.

The bride.

It was all beginning to make a kind of wonderful, miraculous sense. The way she called him Jack. The overwhelming sense of destiny he'd felt the first moment he took her in his arms. The way the years had separated them only to bring them back together when he had more to offer her than a room in a boarding house and a lot of empty dreams.

I SHOULD HAVE KNOWN this was too good to be true. Flynn swallowed hard and touched his arm. "What's wrong?"

He looked at her as if she were an apparition. "You broke your right arm a long time ago."

Her heartbeat accelerated. "I guess it's back to physical therapy for me." Her attempt at lightheartedness failed miserably.

"You also broke your right leg and some ribs."

"You're scaring me, Jack." There was no way for him to know that much about her unless he'd hired a private investigator weeks before they met. Had their "chance meeting" been orchestrated and not as serendipitous as it had seemed? Instead of feeling flattered, she felt uneasy. "If there's something I should know..."

"I don't want to scare you." He took her hand, lacing his fingers with hers.

"Well, you're doing a pretty good job at it."

His chest rose as he took a deep breath. Flynn found it impossible to do the same.

"We've met before, Flynn."

She kissed his cheek. "I think I'd remember meeting you." *He's right. You know he's right . . . you've known it from the start . . .*

"Ten years ago."

"Oh, I don't think so, Flanagan," she said, forcing a laugh. "I was a sheltered little girl. I certainly didn't know any prizefighters."

"I wasn't a prizefighter then. I wasn't much of anything."

A tall boy with sad, dark eyes . . . "I'm sure I'd remember."

"You were married."

Her body jerked with surprise. His grip on her hand tightened, much as it had one day a long time ago.

She looked down at their hands, her eyes burning with tears as memories of a limousine filled with laughter and the smell of flowers surrounded her. "Don't, Jack. Please, don't . . ."

"You hated Jell-O and couldn't wait to have a slice of pizza the second they let you out of there."

"It can't be . . . it's not possible."

He knelt before her, his dark gaze intent upon her. "I'm the one, Flynn."

She was crying openly as she met his eyes, unable to control the emotions that tore at her heart. "You saved my life." Her voice was a whisper. "Your back—" Those scars she'd noticed were badges of courage.

"I didn't care." He cradled her face in his powerful hands. "All I knew was that you had to live. I couldn't let you go."

"But you did." The years fell away from her, and she was once more the terrified child she'd been that last afternoon in the hospital.

"Only to find us a place." He told her about the subway ride to Brooklyn, the desperate search for a place where they could live. A place where they could hide. "It was after four o'clock when I found one. A run-down studio in a six floor walk-up in Bay Ridge. My first mansion didn't look as good to me as that dive." His smile was rueful. "When I got back to the hospital you were gone."

"I didn't want to leave you," she managed. "I wanted to see you again, to thank you, but my uncle—" She wiped her eyes on a corner of the bath towel. "My uncle told me about...about my husband and I..." Her voice trailed off. The memory of that moment when she realized Billy was gone was as sharp and painful today as it had been ten years ago. "The next thing I remember was waking up in a hospital in Switzerland."

"They sedated you?"

She sniffled, wishing she could stop crying long enough to form a sentence. "Out cold. My uncle told me I tried to kill myself."

"With a broken arm and leg?" He looked skeptical.

"I don't remember any of it, but I can't imagine he would lie about something like that." She noticed a small muscle working furiously along the side of Jack's jaw. A frisson of alarm went through her body. "Look, I realize you don't know my uncle. Believe me, he would never say or do anything to hurt me."

"Too bad he didn't feel the same way about me."

"I don't understand."

Jack's laugh was short, bitter. "Let's say we had a confrontational relationship."

Flynn had the sensation of being trapped inside a maze, unable to see her way toward the exit. "I still don't understand."

He met her eyes and didn't allow her to look away. "I went nuts that afternoon when I found you were gone. I trashed the nurses' station."

"What does this have to do with my uncle?" She wished she could stop her limbs from trembling.

"He pressed charges."

"You mean . . . ?"

"Jail. Three years. I got time off for good behavior."

She looked down at her lap as images of her privileged life tumbled inside her brain. "There must be some mistake. My uncle wouldn't do something like that. You saved my life. He would never have done anything to hurt you."

"He was in the chief of staff's office, signing papers. You'd already been hidden away somewhere. I grabbed him by the collar and slugged him. Not that I wasn't heading that way on my own . . ."

"Oh, God." The violence she had sensed in the boy years ago was visible in the face of the man before her today. This wasn't the controlled violence of the boxing ring, but something darker, more primitive. Something intrinsically tied to love and possession and pride.

"You were the best thing that had ever happened to me, and I was willing to do anything to make you happy." He told her about the dreams he'd had for the two of them, the crazy, wonderful dreams that had died that day along with his freedom.

"Don't," she whispered as the memory of that time loomed all around her. "Don't say any more."

"I loved you," he said, his voice cracking. "I wanted to keep you safe."

It wasn't difficult to conjure up that angry young man whose unexpected love had bridged the gap between death and life. And then it was all there inside her, ripping at her heart. Her father...Billy...their friends...those endless days of knowing that nothing would ever bring them back again. Not even if she offered up her life in exchange.

Jack held her close as she cried. His hand cupped her head, making her feel like the protected girl she had been a thousand lifetimes ago.

"It was going to be forever, our marriage. Billy was the only boy I'd ever loved." She brushed her tears away, wishing she could banish the sorrow as easily. "I thought I'd have four children by now and a house in the country and..." Her words trailed off. "I've made my peace with it." She chuckled softly. "I don't know why I'm crying."

He stroked her hair as he had during those days in the hospital.

"I never forgot you," he said, cradling her against his massive chest. "When I was in jail, I'd lie on my cot and picture you with your hair sparkling in the sunshine and your eyes blue as the sky. I'd tell myself I'd find you when I got out. That somehow I'd find you and tell you how much you meant to me."

"I'm here," she whispered. "You can tell me now." She needed to know that she had been important to him in ways that transcended sex.

A hundred different emotions seemed to pass across his rugged face before he spoke again. "I never thought I'd have this chance. You were—" He stopped, gathering his thoughts together. Her heart ached with tenderness. "You were so far above me, Flynn. Everything I'd ever wanted."

She wanted to tell him that she was just a woman, a woman who'd made her own share of mistakes, whose heart had ached with loneliness the same as his. She understood the need to cling to fantasy, to believe in a dream, yet she needed him to know she was far from perfect. The virgin bride he'd held in his arms all those years ago was a thing of the past, a sweet memory but a memory nonetheless.

"You're shaking," he said, drawing her into his arms.

"This whole thing is overwhelming. I don't understand . . . why now? Why have we found each other again?"

"Who knows?" His embrace deepened. "All that matters is that we're together."

"That's too easy, Jack. Things like this don't happen."

He caressed her cheek. "It's happened. We're together."

"I feel as if we're tempting the gods."

"I feel as if the gods are on our side."

She kissed the palm of his hand. "How I wish I could believe that."

"Don't go looking for hidden meanings, Flynn, because there aren't any. We're together. That's enough."

But it wasn't enough. How could it be when the very fact that they had found each other again seemed to defy the odds? Bad things happened to good people. Everyone believed that maxim. Good things happening to good people? Now that was something else entirely. Flynn had grown so used to living behind an emotional suit of armor that the notion of accepting life's blessings seemed fraught with hidden danger.

She met his eyes. "I'm so happy it frightens me, Jack. I never thought I'd feel this way again."

"This time it doesn't have to end."

His expression was serious, his meaning clear.

"Jack, I—"

She was interrupted by a knock at the door and a cheerful "Room service!"

"Breakfast," he said, with an apologetic grin. "It seemed like a good idea at the time."

Flynn scurried into the adjacent dressing room as the door to the hotel suite swung open. In a way she was glad to escape; the conversation had taken a sudden, abrupt downshift into talk of commitment. No one could deny there was an element of destiny to their meeting again after so long. She had never spent a great deal of time musing over fate or kismet or whatever the trendy term for luck was these days. But even she couldn't turn away from the fact that some force beyond the usual had seen fit to reunite her with the man who had saved her life ten years ago.

She rummaged through a stack of clean clothes hidden away in a built-in cupboard in the dressing room. Briefs, and T-shirt, swimming trunks—perfect. A pure white shirt of luxurious Egyptian cotton. She slid her arms into the sleeves, sighing with pleasure at the silky feel of the material. The shirt dangled to the midpoint of her thighs, and she rolled the long sleeves up to her elbow. The shirt held the faintest trace of his scent. She wrapped her arms around her chest and gloried in the feeling of comfort, of security, his scent evoked inside her.

She listened to Jack thank the waiter. How far he'd come from the raw and angry young man she'd met ten years ago—and yet how much of that young man still remained. The combination of raw male strength and human vulnerability overwhelmed what few defenses she had left.

He tapped on the bathroom door. "All clear."

She glided out into the sitting room as if she were clad in an Yves Saint Laurent. The look in his eyes as he took in her outfit pleased her female heart. She felt young and hopeful and deeply, passionately happy for the first time in her adult life. She strolled over to the beautifully set table near the sliding glass doors and peeked under a silver dome.

"Eggs Benedict." She glanced over at Jack as he approached. "How did you know I love this?"

"I didn't." He held Flynn's chair as she sat down. "I asked myself what's the classiest breakfast there is and I ordered it."

She leaned across the table and lifted the other silver dome. "Ham and eggs?"

"Where I come from, that's gourmet fare." He took his seat. "What you see is all there is, Flynn."

She touched his hand. "I like what I see."

He poured her a cup of coffee. His enormous hands looked awkward and sweet against the fragile china.

"There's a lot you don't know about me, Flynn."

Their fingers brushed as she accepted the coffee from him. A simple touch—yet one she felt from her head to her feet.

"I'm a good listener," she said.

"You won't like what you hear."

"There are things about my past you won't like either, Jack." That dark period where she would do anything to avoid another night of aching loneliness seemed part of another lifetime.

Her words seemed to unsettle him, and his eyes narrowed as he watched her.

"They went hard on me in jail," he said finally, "and I fought them every step of the way. I had my nose broken three times the first year, and I deserved it each time. I've got a lousy temper, and it's taken me almost thirty years to get a handle on it."

"Through boxing?"

"It saved my life." His grin was swift and off center. "Probably saved a few other people's, too."

She must have looked shocked because he started to laugh.

"That was a joke, Flynn."

She swallowed a sip of coffee. "I wasn't sure."

"It wasn't far from the truth, though."

"Somehow I didn't think so."

She listened as he told her about growing up near Bed-Stuy, about being the black sheep in a family of black sheep, about being out-of-sync with the rest of the world.

"I wanted everything," he said, pushing his chair back and standing up. "I wanted to get the hell out of the city. I wanted money and respect and a big house on a hill somewhere."

It takes a heart to cry...they say I don't have one...

"Trouble was, I could only think of one way to get all those things." He turned toward the sliding doors that looked out over the bay. "I robbed a deli." He paused. "At gunpoint."

Her sharp intake of breath didn't go unnoticed.

"Still feel the same way about me, Flynn?"

She rose and walked over to where he stood. "You were young and scared. I can understand that." *I've made mistakes, too, Jack. I'm not going to judge you.*

"You don't understand anything." He turned and gripped her by the forearms and once again she saw the ghost of the scared and angry boy he'd been—and, in many ways, still was. "I liked it, Flynn. I liked that feeling of power . . . knowing that I could walk into a room and beat the hell out of every man in it if I wanted to." He told her about the store he had robbed less than an hour before her accident, about the black rage that had propelled him at the hospital, about fighting his way in and out of jail.

"And boxing helped you get rid of that anger?"

He started to laugh. "Let's say it redirected it."

"Still the angry young man?" She tried to keep her tone light and easy but failed miserably. His words scared her, and she couldn't hide it.

"Still angry, but not so young anymore. Boxing helped but it didn't make the problem go away." She followed him back to the table, and they took their seats again. "I'd probably be in the slammer right now if it hadn't've been for Oscar."

"Oscar?" asked Flynn, spearing a piece of egg with her fork.

"Best trainer any heavyweight could hope for."

"He was a prisoner, too?"

"Don't let him hear you say that. He's been in the fight game since he was eleven. Worked his way up from cleaning floors to becoming lightweight champ of 1955. He trained the best. I was lucky enough to be one of them."

"How did he end up in jail?"

"He's one of the good guys. He volunteered his time to help kids like me. He took me under his wing. I don't know where I'd have ended up if he hadn't found me."

"You're a lucky man."

"Yeah," he said, meeting her eyes. "I know that."

"I'd like to meet him."

"You'll probably have your chance any minute. I was on the phone with him when you came out of the bathroom with your new hair color. I bet he's on his way over here right now to read me the riot act for bolting the party last night."

Jack was right. They had barely finished the last of the coffee when a small black man with graying hair swung open the door to Jack's room then strode into the room with the assurance of a man twice his size.

Jack glowered at him. "Don't you know how to knock?"

"Ain't been no need to before today." The man extended his hand to Flynn. "Oscar Davis at your service."

"Flynn Pennington. It's my pleasure."

"The pleasure is definitely mine. I've enjoyed your pretty face looking out at me from a lot of magazines the past few years."

"Knock it off, Oscar," Jack said. "I think she's heard it all before."

"That doesn't mean I don't like hearing it again." There was something about the dapper older man that had endeared him to her instantly. Possibly it was the very obvious affection he and Jack had for each other.

Oscar winked at her then turned to Jack. "How'd a bum like you get so lucky?"

"I'm sure you'll tell me."

"Why don't I let the *New York Times*, *Nassau News* and *USA Today* do it for me?" He pulled the roll of newspapers from under his arm and spread them out on the table before Jack and Flynn. "Good picture, don't you think?"

Flynn leaped to her feet and stood behind Jack, staring down at the exceptionally candid shot of her and Jack entering the hotel last night. They were both fully clothed. They weren't kissing or fondling or doing anything more risqué than holding hands. Yet the bloom of sexuality was all over them. Even in black and white, the photograph exuded eroticism.

Her cheeks blazed. All across the United States, people were drinking their morning coffee and speculating on what exactly had happened in that hotel room last night.

"This is terrible," she moaned. "Everyone will know."

Jack eyed her with curiosity. "You're not attached to anyone?" She shook her head. "Neither am I. Let them write what they want."

"I'm not accustomed to having my private life made public."

Oscar guffawed. "In the business you're in, darlin', every move you make is public. You should be used to it by now."

She shook her head, cheeks blazing. Even during the darkest hour of her self-esteem, she had managed to keep her indiscretions very private. And now here she was with a man who meant so much to her, and their feelings were plastered across the front pages of newspapers coast to coast. Some enterprising reporter was bound to look more deeply and dredge up the accident, and she didn't know if she could bear reliving the past.

Especially not now when her future seemed so bright.

"Isn't there something we can do?" she asked Jack, knowing as well as anybody how all-powerful the American gossip media was.

"Ignore them," said Jack. "They won't go away, but they will get bored. It's worked for me."

What he said was right in theory, but Flynn knew gossip grew exponentially. A great story about one famous person spread quickly; a great story about two famous people spread like the Johnstown Flood.

"He's right," said Oscar, helping himself to a croissant from the wicker basket in the center of the table. "The more you fight, the more they write. Live your life and let the rest of it go."

Good advice, thought Flynn as she studied the newspaper photos. She hoped Oscar was right.

ALISTAIR CHAMBERS poured himself another cup of decaffeinated coffee and leaned back in his chair.

"Well?" Ryder waved the newspaper photograph in his mentor's face. "Do you see what I'm talking about?"

"All I see are two attractive young people having a romantic rendezvous."

Ryder slammed the newspaper down next to Alistair's plate of cholesterol-free imitation eggs and butterless English muffins. "Are you blind? The evidence is right there in front of you."

"You're letting your imagination run wild."

Ryder took another sip of lousy coffee and grimaced. "Something bad's going down, Alistair. I can feel it."

"Gut instinct has served you well through the years, but I wouldn't put all my faith in it."

Ryder hesitated. What he was thinking sounded crazy even to him. Alistair would probably have him sent away for a long rest. "Remember when President Scott died?"

Chambers nodded. "I was in London. The stock market plummeted. Whisper 'conspiracy' around financial men and they fall to their knees in fear."

Ryder took a deep breath. "I think they were right."

"While I might agree with you on the Kennedy assassination, there is nothing to suggest anything other than the aneurysm reported in the autopsy."

"Have you seen the autopsy report?"

Chambers shook his head. "I'm sorry to appear callous, but while I mourned the loss of your leader, I had no interest in reading the medical reports."

"You should have." Not long after Mary Flynn's accident, Ryder had spent five hours locked away in the archives at the Capitol reading everything there was on her father's death. And when he was finished doing that, he delved back into Frederick Scott's health records for the five years before that. Nowhere—*nowhere*—was there any medical evidence of a condition that could predispose the president to a lethal aneurysm.

"Isn't that the nature of the beast?" Alistair said after listening to Ryder's story. "A silent killer."

"You don't get what I'm saying." Ryder kicked back his chair and paced the terrace once again. "There was no physical evidence of a weakness in the blood vessels in Frederick Scott's brain."

"You mean *before*."

Check and mate. "No, Chambers, I mean *after*."

"You're positive?"

"Damn straight I am."

"Why wasn't the information made public?"

"Sealed documents." Luckily for Ryder, he knew how to circumvent minor details like that.

"This doesn't make sense, my boy."

"It will once I tell you who ordered the documents sealed."

It was one of those moments that don't happen often enough in an average lifetime. The look on Alistair's face would have made Ryder's week if the subject had been less important.

"Hugh Scott?" asked Chambers.

"Dead on," said Ryder.

THAT AFTERNOON Hugh Scott was an unhappy man.

He stared down at the newspaper photograph on his burled wood desk. He was long accustomed to seeing Mary Flynn's face looking out at him from the pages of glossy magazines and television commercials as she exhorted consumers to spend more money.

The shot was candid. The meaning, crystal clear. Mary Flynn and Jack Flanagan had defied the odds and rediscovered each other. In a long and careful career, Hugh Scott had rarely left a loose end dangling to trip him up at a later date.

Only one time, ten years ago. Oh, it wasn't that he regretted the fact that Mary Flynn had survived the accident. He loved the girl as much as he was capable of loving anyone, but trusting that she knew nothing about the circumstances surrounding her father's death was akin to playing Russian roulette with all chambers loaded. After the accident that took her husband's life, she had let much of her past drift away from her, willingly buried deep inside her subconscious with memories of her tragic wedding day.

It would take something extraordinary to unlock those secrets.

Something like the reappearance of Jack Flanagan in her life.

Across from him, Thomas Judd lit a cigarette. "Interesting, no?"

Scott met his personal assistant's curious gaze. "I fail to see what you find amusing."

"This is a bit of a coincidence, isn't it?" Judd continued, pressing an obvious point. "What were the chances those two would meet again?"

"A million to one," Scott said quietly.

"Something has to be done."

"Obviously."

"Any ideas?"

Scott glanced over at the medals and citations hanging on the wall next to him. "A few."

Judd puffed furiously on his cigarette. "Going to share any with me?"

"In due time." He feigned boredom and riffled through a stack of documents next to the newspaper. "I expect the nuclear fusion treaty on my desk before five o'clock."

He had to commend Judd; the years had served the younger man well. Ten years ago Judd would have stormed from the room at such an abrupt dismissal. Now he understood the art of patience. Scott would take his assistant into his confidence eventually, but he preferred to be the one to determine exactly when.

His thoughts returned to his niece.

"Ah, Mary," he said, refolding the newspaper and sliding it into his desk drawer. "Are you going to force my hand at such a late date?"

When she survived the "accident" all those years ago, Scott had considered his options. He had come too far to take a chance at exposure now. There was no way of knowing exactly how much her husband William Pennington had confided in her, but Scott knew his niece well enough to believe that had she any inkling of the truth, she would have been the first to blow the whistle on him.

Her selective amnesia had been a blessing. Even after he'd told her about Billy, huge gaps remained in her memory—and did so, he believed, until this very day. She had done her level best to block out that terrible portion of her life, and do so in many ways he did not approve of. Strange to say, but he loved the girl in his own way and looked forward to the day she would marry again and have children to carry on the Scott family tradition.

Unfortunately the hand of fate had positioned a new player on the game board. Wild Man Flanagan. *Wild Card.*

Yes, Mr. Flanagan was definitely the wild card. The key that could unlock the secrets buried in Mary's subconscious these ten years past.

The *x* factor that could destroy everything Hugh Scott had labored long to build for himself.

Flanagan was an ignorant fool and, as such, would ordinarily be too insignificant to merit Scott's notice. But Flanagan was also the catalyst that just might unlock Mary's memories—and reveal the secret Scott would kill again to protect.

Yes, he thought, staring out the window at Lake Geneva glittering below. It was time to act.

Chapter Nine

Oscar was a delight—although, at the moment, Jack didn't seem to think so.

After breakfast Jack excused himself to give a series of phone interviews, but he still found time to cast a baleful glance in his trainer's direction.

"Don't you have some place to go?" he growled as Oscar poured more coffee for Flynn.

"Keeping Flynn company."

Flynn flashed Jack a wicked grin. "Oscar's promised to tell me all of your darkest secrets."

"Don't bother," said Jack, kissing Flynn on the top of her head. "I've already told all of them."

Flynn laughed and watched Jack as he left the room. How amazing to believe she had spent the night wrapped in the strong arms of the man who'd saved her life so many years before.

She turned back to Oscar, only to find his dark brown eyes watchful and concerned.

"Serious?" he asked.

She hesitated, then opted for total honesty. "For me, yes."

Oscar grabbed himself a sweet roll and slathered it with butter. "Twenty-four hours ago I would have paid you anything to leave town."

"Twenty-four hours ago you wouldn't have had to. This was totally unexpected."

Oscar chewed his roll thoughtfully. "Tell me if I'm wrong, but it seems to these eyes that there's more between the two of you than twenty-four hours."

"That obvious?"

"I know that boy as well as I could know a son. In all these years I never once saw him look at anybody the way he looked at you this morning."

She put down her coffee cup and met Oscar's direct gaze with one of her own. "He saved my life."

"Say what?"

She touched his hand. "He saved my life." She started to tell him a condensed version of the story when his expression changed.

"You're the bride."

A brief smile touched her lips. "You know the story?"

"Chapter and verse. Wouldn't think a kid like that would fall so hard, but there's no tellin' when it comes to love."

"We only knew each other a week, Oscar. I wouldn't call it love."

"He said you made him feel like he could do anything. If that ain't love, what is?"

She thought for a moment. "I don't know." It seemed odd to talk about love. She'd never imagined she would know that emotion again. The years had brought with them an aching emptiness that she had sought to fill time and time again in the arms of dif-

ferent men. It had never worked. On her twenty-fifth
birthday she decided the answer rested within herself
and she looked inward. That hadn't worked, either.
How could it when her public image was that of a cool
postmodern woman, while her private image was that
of a frightened child?

The past two years had been spent in a dizzying
whirl of activity. She was booked three years in ad-
vance by major magazines around the world. She went
to the best parties, stayed at the finest resorts, spent
time with the world's wittiest and most influential
players, and still the emptiness inside. Last night, in
Jack's strong arms, was the first time she felt whole.

Oscar's voice snapped her back to the present. "I
don't want that boy hurt," he was saying, his voice
stern but compassionate. "You can do more damage
to him than Muhammad Ali in his prime without even
liftin' up one of those pretty little hands of yours."

"I wouldn't hurt him, Oscar. I—"

"What?" Oscar pressed. "Do you love him?"

"I—I don't know." She forced a laugh. "I mean, it
has been only twenty-four hours."

"Not to him it hasn't. To him it's been a lifetime."

"I doubt if he's been celibate all these years, Oscar,
while he pined away for me."

"There's a big difference between having sex and
making love, Flynn. I'm real surprised I have to tell
you that."

"You don't," she said quietly.

"Retirement's gonna be real rough on the kid. It's
not easy to be unemployed just before your thirtieth
birthday."

"Financially he's okay, isn't he?"

"Takes more than a few million to soothe a man's soul. Especially a man with a soul as troubled as Jack's."

She picked up a newspaper at random from the stack atop the table and flipped to the sports page. "'Flanagan Staggers Curtis with Blow—Super Fight, Super Fists.'" She looked up at Oscar. "He's only hitting his prime now. All the sports writers say so. Why doesn't he fight a few years longer if it's that important to him?" While she'd certainly rather he never see the inside of a boxing ring again, she understood the need to follow your heart.

"The mob."

She froze, hand on her coffee cup. "What?"

"The mob," Oscar repeated. "We kept him clean and they don't like it. They wouldn't mind one last bout so they can get a piece of him before he's out for good. Kid's worth a whole lot of money to the right promoter."

"Is he in any danger?"

"Nothing we can't handle. Sooner or later they'll give up."

"He wouldn't fight again, would he?" The thought of the man she'd loved last night stepping into the ring filled her with dread. The thought of the mob exercising control over him filled her with terror.

Oscar's response was swift and fierce. "Over my dead body."

She thought about Jack, about the controlled violence, the physical nature of his personality. "I can't imagine him sitting behind a desk somewhere. What exactly does an ex-prizefighter do with the rest of his life?"

"All depends how quick you get out. The boy's lucky: he's still got his wits about him, and he's not too bad to look at." He shook his head. "You listen to Muhammad Ali today and it's about enough to break your heart. I want it to be different for Johnny. We got offers stacked as high as the ceiling back in New York." Oscar polished off his coffee and grinned. "Hell, we could start him out on the rubber-chicken circuit tonight if he wanted to."

"The rubber-chicken circuit?"

"Kiwanis clubs, Masons, college campuses—that sort of thing."

"What does he want?"

"Beats me. I was hoping you might be the one to figure that out."

She looked down for a second. "I don't know exactly what's going to happen between us, Oscar. This is still extremely new."

He leaned across the table and riveted her with a forbidding look. "I want to ask you a favor."

"I'm not sure I'm going to like it."

"I'm not sure I'm going to like asking it, but it's gotta be asked for the boy's sake."

She swallowed hard. "Shoot."

"I want you to make me a promise that the moment you discover the boy isn't what you're lookin' for, you'll get out of his life clean and simple."

Her back stiffened. "I'm not with Jack for his money, Oscar, if that's what's worrying you." She quoted an impressive seven-digit figure and waited while it sank in. "Annual income, Oscar. Mine."

"I'm impressed."

"Good. I don't need anyone else's fame or money." She had plenty of both commodities on her own, for whatever good it did her. "I'm interested only in Jack." *Well, there you are, Mary. Now you've said it right out loud.* Had any affair started as oddly as this one?

"I'm not worryin' about his bank balance, Flynn. I'm worried about his heart. If there's anyone else in your life, do us all a favor and head out that door."

She patted Oscar's hand. "I know you love him, but you can't control his life the way you control his career. You're just going to have to roll with the punches this time, Oscar."

"You're a real nice girl," he said, "but I got me a feeling that nothin' good's going to come of this. Nothing good at all."

OSCAR LEFT ABOUT AN HOUR LATER. Jack finished his radio interviews and sifted through a stack of requests a foot high from photojournalists, sports reporters and groupies to come down to the ballroom and hold an impromptu news conference.

"You probably should," Flynn said as she doubled one of his belts around her slender waist. "You have to think about your future."

He pulled her into his arms. "I am thinking about my future." He kissed the side of her throat exposed by the open shirt. "I can't believe how terrific you look in that outfit."

Flynn laughed and pirouetted for him. "All it takes is a little ingenuity." She had layered his Egyptian cotton shirt over the slinky mini she'd worn the night before, then belted the whole thing low over her hips.

"I'll pick up a pair of sandals in one of the boutiques off the lobby and I'm all set." She kissed his mouth lightly, touching the tip of her index finger to the cleft in his chin. "Besides, I don't want to advertise the fact we spent the night together."

His brows slid into a scowl. "Ashamed of something, Flynn?"

"No." Her answer was from the heart. For the first time in years she wasn't ashamed of anything at all. "But I would like to retain whatever we can of our privacy." She'd spent her first sixteen years as a public person; now, as an adult, her face was still public property. Her life, however, was another story.

Hand-in-hand they left the hotel. Jack had sent a member of his staff to retrieve her luggage from her hotel and deposit it in his suite.

"I have to be back in New York by tomorrow night," she said as they crossed the curving drive toward his car. She hated the intrusion of the real world, but it was unavoidable.

"Business?"

"A shoot at South Street Seaport the next morning."

He didn't look happy about it. "Call in sick."

"No, Jack."

He stopped and looked down at her. "You don't need the money. I'll take care of you."

"I can take care of myself. I always have and I don't intend to stop now." *Even if I just might be falling in love with you again.* She softened at the look on his face. "Let's be equals in this, Jack. Let's be together only because that's where we want to be."

And that's when she saw the man he would have been if life had been kinder to him from the start. The vulnerability in his dark eyes was her undoing. Right there, in the middle of the street separating the hotel from the parking lot, she held him close, praying that something as simple as a kiss could convey all that she wanted to say to him.

JACK'S FEELINGS terrified him. She'd reached inside his heart, scaled his defenses, done the one thing nobody had ever been able to do: made him feel vulnerable. Time stretched around him as they embraced, and he didn't know if he held Flynn in his arms or the bride of long ago. He started to speak, to try somehow to find the words to explain the emotions battling inside him, when he became aware of a noise.

A low rumble beneath his feet, a roar then—

"Did I hurt you?" He had pushed her to the ground then covered her body with his at the approach of the car. He helped Flynn to her feet at the side of the road. She was covered in sandy dirt, disheveled, and scared.

"I—I don't know." She dusted off her bottom and gave him a shaky smile. "That was some kiss, fella."

He found it impossible to smile back at her. "That son of a bitch almost killed us."

"Probably drunk," said Flynn, frowning up at him as he wiped blood from his already battered cheekbone.

He stepped back into the street and peered in the direction the car had vanished. "If I get my hands on that—"

"He's long gone, Jack." Flynn popped up at his side and took his hand, tugging him back toward the parking lot. "Forget it."

He couldn't. "Did you see what kind of car it was?"

She shook her head. "I was otherwise occupied."

Now that, he couldn't ignore. A smile tugged at the corners of his mouth. "We'll have to be more careful."

Her beautiful blue eyes glowed. "Or more discreet."

He'd rented a small Mercedes convertible, and Flynn was duly taken with it. In short order they were buckled in, and he headed out for a drive.

They crossed the bridge and ended up in the shopping district on Nassau. It was more choked with people than lower Manhattan on a Monday morning. He left the car in a tiny lot a good distance away, and they joined the crowds of tourists who were all searching for the best bargains in town.

He had never been with a woman who understood herself and her own style the way Flynn did. Watching her toy with a scarf or angle a simple sailor's cap on her head until it showed her spectacular face to best advantage was mesmerizing. Her hair was pulled into a ponytail, her face free of makeup. She was the most beautiful woman he had ever known.

"I think we've been spotted," Flynn said as they lingered at the window of a jewelry store. "We're being followed."

Jack looked over his shoulder and saw a gaggle of giggling girls watching them from a not-so-discreet distance away. He grinned at them. They didn't grin back. That's when it hit him. "They're watching you!"

"All little girls want to grow up and be models these days."

He knew Flynn was famous in her field, but he hadn't really made the connection until this moment as he stood next to her while she signed autographs for a score of admirers. He had thought of her as "his." The fact that she had a life beyond this moment hadn't penetrated until now as he watched her charm her already-adoring fans.

"This could take some getting used to," he said when they were finally alone again. "I didn't know I'd have to share you with your groupies."

"Turnabout's fair play, Flanagan. Oscar told me you have four international fan clubs."

"That's different." Unfortunately he couldn't explain how or why it was different, just that it was. He'd never given a damn before if the woman he was seeing had a life beyond their relationship. He'd always assumed they did and let it go at that. With Flynn it was different. He knew all about liberation and women's rights and the need for balance in life. None of it mattered when he looked at her beautiful face. He wanted to spirit her away to some distant place and keep her safe and happy.

And his alone.

"Come on," he said. "Let's go back to the hotel."

"I haven't finished shopping."

"Yes, you have."

"Caveman techniques are a bit outdated, Flanagan."

He grinned and kissed her right there in the middle of the street.

Her eyes glittered in the Caribbean sun. "Outdated and *very* effective."

They headed back for the hotel.

In Geneva Hugh Scott hung up the telephone and leaned back in his leather chair.

Thomas Judd tapped impatiently on the desktop with his index finger. "What happened?"

"All went well," said Scott. "The first warning has been issued."

A car had scraped close enough to Jack Flanagan to peel a layer of skin off his biceps. Flanagan, it seemed, had brushed it off as the work of a rotten driver.

Well and good.

The second warning should come as quite a surprise.

"Just leave Mary alone," he warned Judd. "She is not to be hurt in this."

"You didn't feel that way ten years ago. Why the change of heart?" Judd always spoke his mind. It was both his best and worst trait.

"Because she no longer poses a threat." They'd covered that ground before. Spilling her blood would serve no useful purpose and would reduce the entire Scott clan by half. The thought of bringing his illustrious clan closer to extinction was unconscionable to Hugh. She was their only hope for progeny, for continuance. For the things he'd worked hard to preserve to go forward into another century of greatness.

"As you wish," said Judd at last, rising to leave the room. "But there will be no reprieve this time should your niece's memory return *in toto*."

"And that, Thomas, is my problem. Not yours. The plan continues per my original orders."

DONALD REID HAD EVERYTHING a man could want. *Almost*.

He had a beautiful wife and three beautiful children. He had a steady job and a little money in the bank. But the one thing he didn't have was self-respect.

Yeah, he knew he'd done pretty well, considering the fact he was only a journeyman sportswriter. The *Florida Intelligencer* was a bottom-of-the-barrel newspaper, and with each year that passed, it seemed more likely he would end his days writing copy about the Mets' spring training camp, instead of the important stories his colleagues managed to draw.

The only reason he'd managed to snag the Fight of the Century was because Joe Lawson, head sportswriter, had had a gall bladder attack during a seafood dinner on the pier.

Not that Reid had always wanted to be a sportswriter. Hell, during his salad days he'd dreamed of being a one-man Woodward and Bernstein, exposing government corruption, political machinations and conspiracies. Where the older reporters had cut their professional teeth during the tumultuous years after the Kennedy assassinations, Donald Reid had taken the Frederick Scott episode as his own cause.

And why not? Fate had put him right in the center of things, almost from the beginning. He was the only reporter on the scene when Mary Flynn had her wedding day accident. Not that he'd realized she was Mary Flynn back then, mind you, but the coincidence struck him as meaningful, just the same.

There was a reason for it, but he hadn't been able to come up with it at the time; now, ten years later, he still couldn't.

But still it lingered, gnawing at his insides like a disease. One, unfortunately, still without a cure.

Back home in Florida he had stacks of paper on every aspect of Scott's death. He had elaborately executed diagrams that detailed Scott's activities on the day of his death, with parallel diagrams for each member of his staff. He'd even come in contact with a young guy from some government agency who'd spent as much time in the New York Public Library as he did.

Reid had never bought the story behind Mary Flynn Scott's accident. The parallels between the post-Kennedy period and the post-Scott period were too striking to be ignored. A young man. An unexpected demise. The subsequent deaths of everyone close to the investigations. The accident that had taken away Mary Flynn's young husband just as he was embarking on a political career that had the potential to be as successful as his late father's. The fact that his late father had been the head of the commission investigating Frederick Scott's death seemed to have been lost on everyone but Reid. A swimming accident had been highly unlikely for a man on the second team for the summer Olympics of 1948.

You'd have to have cement for brains to miss the importance of it all.

And you'd have to have cement for brains to miss the importance of Mary Flynn and Wild Man Flanagan. He couldn't quite put his finger on it, but he knew they belonged together. In fact, he'd bet his notebook that he'd seen them together a long time ago.

Like right around the time Mary was in the hospital and Flanagan was a kid looking for trouble.

He watched as Flanagan and Mary Flynn strolled through the hotel lobby and headed toward the penthouse elevator.

First, the Fight of the Century, now—just maybe—the Story of the Century.

Donald Reid raised his glass of rum in the air and laughed out loud.

Maybe his luck was finally going to change.

THERE ARE THINGS SAID in the heart of the night that are better left unsaid, but lovers rarely possess that kind of wisdom.

Flynn was no exception.

As she lay in Jack's arms on their second night together, she was overcome with the realization that they existed out of time and place. That their second night was measured only by the world and not by the heart. For in her heart she had been his forever.

Jack had made love to her with passion and tenderness. The excitement was no less intense than it had been the night before, but this time the earth-shattering violence of the explosion inside her body was tempered with a sweetness that turned the act of love into something approaching a sacrament. The bond between them was powerful, as much a bond of the spirit as it was a bond of the flesh. In his arms she lost track of the years they had lost; their time apart seemed of little consequence when compared to the sense of destiny, of rightness, in their coming together once again.

He brought back the girl she'd thought long vanished, that sense of optimism and hope she'd lost in the accident. He made her feel safe and secure, protected and loved—all of the things she'd never believed possible again in her lifetime. How she wished she had something of value to offer him, something that would define the indefinable emotions that made her love him.

"You okay?" His voice was a pleasant rumble against the curve of her ear.

"Fine." She turned her head slightly and looked into his dark eyes. "Why do you ask?"

"I heard you sigh."

She propped herself up on one elbow and rested a hand against his chest. "I was wishing I had some way to show you what you mean to me."

He chuckled and reached for her, but she raised her hand to stop him.

"I'm serious, Flanagan." She looked away for a moment, but his intensity drew her back. "I wish you had been the first, that there had been no others before you." Her voice broke. *Foolish little Mary... the girl who would wait until she got married...* "I wish I could give that gift to you."

JACK DIDN'T SAY ANYTHING. He didn't touch her. The distance between them seemed miles to him, instead of the scant inch or two it was. He wasn't a fool; he knew that expecting virginity from a twenty-nine-year-old woman was no more logical than expecting the same from a twenty-nine-year-old man.

But logic had little to do with the feelings she had stirred up inside him from the very start. Feelings so fierce, so primal, that he was almost ashamed that in the waning years of the twentieth century a man could still feel rage at the thought that he wasn't the first.

"I've done things I'm not very proud of, Flanagan."

Shut up. I don't want to hear this.

"There have been men along the way..." She looked at him for encouragement. He offered none. "I—I was a virgin when I married Billy. I had believed in saving myself for the man I loved, in fidelity, in building something special that would last a lifetime. After he died—" She swallowed hard. "After he died, it seemed that the best part of me had died with him. I hated myself—why had a nobody like me lived through the crash when a man as wonderful as Billy had died? He had so much to offer the world—" Her voice broke. "Everything I believed in seemed ridiculous. The one man I wanted, the one man I loved, was gone and I'd never shared his bed, never known what it was like to wake up in his arms."

He listened, numb with ancient angers, to her story. She had sought solace with other men. She had looked for security in their beds. What she had once believed was the ultimate expression of love and respect became as shallow and commonplace as brushing her teeth. It was a brief, intense period of indiscretion that left her more lost and lonely than she'd been before and from that time on.

"I was stronger than I thought." She shook her head in amazement. "All the old standbys were right there inside me waiting to be called upon." Self-respect. Intelligence. Her belief in God and the natural order of things. The fact that, for her, sex without love wasn't worth the trade-off.

"Talk to me, Flanagan." Her voice spanned the distance between them. "Don't shut me out."

He had no experience in talking to a woman. In the brief time he'd known Flynn, both then and now, he had talked more about what was truly important than he had at any other time in his life. Sharing his body had always come easily; sharing his soul was uncharted territory. But he'd never backed down from a challenge in his life. What he said to her now would set the tone for their future.

He pulled her as close as he could, until her body and his were almost joined. He wished he had the words to explain the fears rushing through him—and the almost savage pride that this woman was his. "I'm the last," he said at last. "You belong to me now."

She nodded and he thought he saw the ghost of a smile play upon her lips. "The very last, Flanagan." She opened for him and welcomed him inside her body. "There's only you."

Chapter Ten

For the first time in her life, Flynn forgot about everything but the pursuit of happiness. Jack ignited something inside her heart, a fire that burned away sorrow and fear and everything but the pure joy in living.

Unfortunately Flynn also forgot that she was scheduled to take the seven a.m. flight back to New York that second morning and not the eight a.m. flight. When the telephone clerk informed her that all remaining flights that day were booked, she saw her career going up in a puff of smoke.

"What am I going to do?" She turned to Jack. "I've never missed an assignment in my life."

"You could stay here."

How tempting that sounded. "I'd love to," she said, "and I may end up doing exactly that if I can't find a way out of here."

"But you'd rather go back to New York."

"I'd rather stay with you, Flanagan, but I can't."

He reached over to where she stood by the nightstand and slid his hand up along the length of her thigh. Her breath caught at his touch; she couldn't have moved if she wanted to. She'd never believed the stories about women in thrall to the power of a man. She'd never known the pleasure of surrender until now. If he asked her again, she would do the unthinkable and stay right there, responsibility be damned.

But he didn't ask.

What he did was hire a private jet to fly the two of them, plus Oscar, back to New York so Flynn could meet her obligations.

"He's quite a man," she said to Oscar as the plane took to the air. "He conjured this up from nowhere." Who would have imagined a man like Flanagan had a Rolodex inside his head and could instantly call up the number of his friendly, local charter plane company. "This is almost wonderful enough to make me forget I'm afraid of flying."

"We use this outfit a lot. Johnny found 'em. The boy's got himself a damn good brain, even if he don't always believe it." Oscar cast a baleful glance at the earth disappearing beneath the wing. "Put together a real estate deal sweeter than Donald Trump."

Jack was in the rear of the plane, talking with the navigator.

"Is that what he'll do now? Real estate?"

"Beats me."

"He won't fight again, will he?" In boxing, retirements were notoriously changeable. Jack had already told her all about Muhammad Ali and Sugar Ray Leonard and many other fighters who had had multiple farewell bouts, complete with press and fanfare.

"There's no telling," said Oscar as Jack approached them. "All depends on which way the wind blows."

"Winds are blowing nice and calm." Jack sat down next to Flynn and took her hand. "Navigator says we'll have a smooth flight all the way up to New York."

"Don't recall seeing that particular guy before," said Oscar.

Flynn noted the look in his brown eyes and realized the topic of Jack's future was tabled for the time being.

"Dave got sick last night," Jack answered, motioning for the attendant to start serving. "The replacement seems pretty sharp. Filed a flight plan that avoids some squalls off the Carolinas."

Flynn was no stranger to luxury, but even she was duly impressed by the attentive service they received twenty-five thousand feet above the earth. Fresh-squeezed orange juice, Kona coffee, the flakiest brioches imaginable. She was in ecstasy. The men tucked into steak and eggs. She longed to launch into a lecture on cholesterol and fat intake, but they looked so happy with their macho breakfast that she decided to save the health report for when they were earth-bound.

Afterward the trays disappeared as quickly as they had arrived. She curled up against Jack's side and did her best to nap, but despite the smoothness of the flight, she was acutely aware of the fact that she was five miles above the earth. She was finally sinking into sleep when the pilot's voice crackled over the intercom.

"If you'll look out the right-hand window, you can clearly see the Washington Monument and the dome of the Capitol."

Flynn groaned and squeezed her eyes shut. The last thing she wanted was to see her old hometown from that altitude.

"What?" Oscar's voice pierced the quiet of the cabin. "You're kidding me!"

"Not about that." Jack sounded amused. "Ask her."

She opened one eye. Oscar was staring at her as if he'd never seen her before. "You lived in the White House?"

"Guilty."

"I thought Johnny was lying."

"Afraid he told you the truth this time, Oscar."

"Your folks on staff there?"

She winked at Flanagan. "You might say that. My dad kind of ran the place."

Oscar looked from Flynn to Jack then back again. "You don't mean—"

"Yes, I do. My dad was Frederick Scott."

Oscar's face registered both surprise and sorrow, and Flynn found herself responding in kind.

"He was a great man," said Oscar. "I miss him."

"So do I." His simple words touched her deeply. "He would have been a wonderful president, if he'd only had time."

They talked for a few moments about the thwarted promise of her father's presidency and then, to Flynn's amazement, she found herself remembering the sweet times and not the sad.

"It was like a wonderful playground," she said dreamily. "I had my own horse on the East Lawn, four dogs and, best of all, my dad worked at home! I couldn't have asked for more."

Of course she could have asked for it to have gone on for much longer than it did, but Flynn tried hard not to ask for what could never be. It was almost enough to be able to share her memories with people who cared.

"You really tried to slide down the laundry chute?" Flanagan's dark blue eyes twinkled with laughter. "I had you pegged for a perfect kid."

"Good, but not perfect," said Flynn. "Having that big old house as my personal castle was too much to resist." She'd also gotten trapped in the ancient dumbwaiter, locked herself out of the house at Camp David, and rattled the rafters when she had a pajama party that spilled over into the Oval Office. "Dad was wonderful. He never raised his voice. He knew how to quell a dozen adolescent girls with just a look." She'd loved him with all her heart and missed him every day of her life. "They do so many wonderful things today with stroke victims. I can't help but wonder if maybe he could have been saved."

"No point thinkin' about that, girl." Oscar reached over and squeezed her hand. "Enjoy the life you've got and keep his memory in your heart. Can't do more than that."

"I—" Flynn stopped, alarmed by a sudden lurch of the plane's slender body. "What was that?"

"Probably an air pocket," said Jack. "Nothing to worry about."

Right on cue the pilot's voice crackled over the intercom once again. "Sorry to bother you, folks, but the seat-belt sign is on again. Looks like we're gonna run into a little clear air turbulence over Baltimore and—"

The plane dipped to the left, shuddered, then seemed to drop a thousand feet. Flynn's stomach dropped along with it.

"Oh, God." Her voice was a strangled moan. "I...hate...flying."

Jack drew her as close as the seat belts would allow. "Nothing's going to happen. The navigator probably has an alternate flight plan all ready to go. It'll be smooth sailing any minute now."

The words were no sooner out of his mouth than the plane bucked like a wild horse. "I hate flying," Flynn groaned. "I hate flying..."

"Another move like that one and I'll be screaming along with you," said Oscar through gritted teeth. At least she wasn't alone with her fear of flying. Jack, however, remained unconcerned.

"We'll be making a landing in Baltimore," said the pilot over the intercom again. "We've lost partial hydraulic power. Expect a bumpy ride, but I assure you there's nothing to worry about."

She grabbed Jack's arm. "What does he mean?"

"Just sit tight. We'll be on the ground before you know it."

"I know this isn't anything...I know planes make emergency landings all the time...I—" Jack leaned over and kissed her. "What was that for?"

"Nothing's going to happen, Flynn. We've got Fate on our side."

The engines whined as the pilot pulled back on the power. The tail dipped low; the nose seemed to shudder then drop forward. Finally the scream of brakes echoed up and down the small cabin.

Flynn didn't dare open her eyes. "Are we dead?"

She took a deep breath and lifted her lids. Flanagan was the first thing she saw. That blessed, beautiful face of his. "Oh, Flanagan, I—" What on earth was happening to her? She had almost said "I love you." They were strangers almost, although she had known him for years. They had shared so little in the framework of a lifetime, yet the past ten years wouldn't have existed had he not pulled her from the edge of death. It was so easy to love him, yet so hard to tell him so.

"I told you it was nothing," said Jack, once more the dominant and confident male animal. "Just a minor glitch."

The pilot apologized profusely for the difficulties. "Damn plane's never had a moment downtime. It's the strangest thing. Can't believe this happened with you on board, Mr. Flanagan."

Jack waved away the apologies. "You got us down safely. That's the important thing. What went wrong?"

"Beats the hell out of me. Looks like either a magneto or one of the hydraulics around the tail rudder. Mechanics are taking it apart now."

"Can we get another plane out?"

"Wish I could help you, Mr. Flanagan, but the navigator begged off. Said he's had enough for one day."

"Smart man," said Oscar. "I think I'll take Amtrak back."

Flynn didn't care for two-hundred-mile-per-hour trains any more than she did five-hundred-mile-per-hour airplanes. "I'd better call the agency and tell them I might not make the shoot tomorrow."

"You won't miss the shoot," said Flanagan. "We'll drive. We'll be back in the city by dinnertime."

"A nice normal car?"

"A Buick," said Flanagan. "You don't get much more normal than that."

"Ground transportation," said Flynn with a sigh of relief. "Perfect!"

JACK RENTED A BUICK as promised, and they dropped Oscar and his luggage off at the nearest Amtrak station. "You sure you don't want a lift?" Jack asked as they shook hands on the platform.

"Got myself looking forward to a train trip," said his trainer, casting a glance toward Flynn who waited in the car. "Besides, I've been around long enough to know when I'm not wanted."

"Smart man."

Oscar's laugh sounded loud in the quiet station. "I think you found yourself the real thing this time around, boy. Don't you go blowing it by treating her like anything less than the genuine article." He gave Jack an awkward hug. "You remember we've got a meeting Friday morning with the brass from that hotshot advertising company. Could mean big bucks for the future."

Jack shook his head. "I'll be there, Oscar, but I'll be damned if I take a bubble bath for anybody."

IN JACK'S OPINION, they hadn't built a car with personality since 1966, and the staid rented Buick was a perfect example. Safe, solid and bland, the car did exactly what it was supposed to do—but with all the excitement of a church supper. The DeLorean had come close to recreating the idiosyncratic muscle cars of the early sixties, but bad press and an elitist price tag had put an end to its dreams of street immortality.

Driving was about freedom. Driving was about the American passion for speed and power. To a kid raised on the streets of Brooklyn, driving was about getting out, getting away, getting even with the fat cats in their Caddy Eldorados and stretch limos who ruled the city.

But even in that sober sedan chugging along on six cylinders, Jack was enjoying the drive up from D.C. Privacy had become a luxury over the years; in that run-of-the-mill Buick he was just another anonymous turnpike commuter on his daily run. No photographers. No reporters. No fans. He could get used to this kind of life.

Next to him, Flynn stirred in her sleep. Oh, yeah— he could get used to this all right. Somewhere around Delaware she had offered to spell him for a while, but by the time they hit South Jersey and he was ready for a break, she was curled next to him in the passenger's seat, napping peacefully. She looked so young as she slept; with her pale golden hair drifting across her delicate face, she was once again the beautiful bride he had fallen in love with all those years ago.

Last night as she lay in his arms, he understood everything there was to know about destiny. She questioned the powers that had seen fit to bring them together again. He thanked those same powers from the bottom of his heart and soul. Life wasn't fair or logical. Anyone who looked for reasons for why things happened the way they did was on a fool's quest.

Jack knew that. He'd railed against fate, cursed the Almighty, brought the wrath of the angels down around his own head when he was young and angry and in jail. To find someone like Flynn only to lose her so quickly—was it any wonder he'd gone out of his head?

He wasn't asking questions now. He wasn't going to waste time looking for meanings that weren't there. He was going to grab life with both hands and hold Flynn as close to his heart as he could.

And he wasn't going to let her go.

FLYNN WOKE UP HALFWAY through the Holland Tunnel between New Jersey and New York. They were stuck in traffic under the Hudson River on a hot summer day and not even that was enough to dim her high spirits. She was happy, rested and extremely hungry.

Jack laughed and glanced at the digital clock on the dashboard. "It's not even five o'clock yet, Flynn."

She cuddled as close to him as her seat belt would allow. "I'm on Caribbean time."

"The Caribbean's in the same time zone as New York."

She made a face. "I never knew you were such a stickler for detail, Flanagan. I may have to rethink this whole—"

He kissed her soundly. She felt his kiss in every cell of her body—but especially in her heart.

"That's wonderful, Flanagan," she said with a sigh, "but I'm still hungry." She thought for a moment. "I know a wonderful Chinese restaurant on the East Side. We could call for take-out." She looked at him. "You do like Szechuan, don't you?"

He shrugged. "I can take it or leave it."

"We're going to have to have a talk about that. I can't live without Szechuan food."

They exited the tunnel and he headed uptown. "I was thinking more like Italian food."

She glanced at him. "Anything in particular?"

"Pizza."

"I love pizza."

His expression was carefully bland. "I remember."
Pizza... The first thing I want when I'm released is pizza....

"There's a great little Italian place off Columbus Avenue."

"I know an even greater Italian place." He paused a beat. "In Brooklyn."

"Where?"

"Brooklyn."

She stared at him. "You're kidding!"

"You make it sound like Mars, Flynn."

"I've never been to Brooklyn."

"You've gotta be kidding."

She shook her head. "I've lived a sheltered life, Flanagan." *And a lonely one.*

"It's a rough neighborhood we're going to," he said, glancing at her.

"Where you grew up?"

He laughed. "Not quite. We're going to Bay Ridge."

She thought for a moment. "*Saturday Night Fever* country. Tony Manero. Discos and gold chains."

"And the best pizza in the country."

"Lead on, Flanagan," she said, curling up again on the passenger's seat. "I'm all yours."

HE WAS DIFFERENT SOMEHOW in Brooklyn. More comfortable, less guarded. His laugh was louder, his movements quicker. He came to life on the street, surrounded by people who understood exactly what it meant to get out—and then to come back home again.

They devoured a pepperoni pizza at Romeo's, a storefront tucked in between a lingerie shop and a finance company.

"I'm trying to imagine you here," she said a little later as they walked back to the rented car. "You were so angry, Flanagan. I'd like to see your old neighborhood."

They climbed into the car and he started the engine. She touched his arm. "Please."

"I don't think so."

"I want to know more about you, Flanagan." *I want to know what made you the man you are.*

"The old neighborhood doesn't exist anymore," he said as he moved into the flow of traffic. "Urban blight, overcrowding, gentrification—you'd be hard-pressed to recreate the way it used to be." Nothing had stood still in the ten years since they had last seen each other—not in their lives or the life of the city.

Brooklyn was a maze of narrow streets, broad avenues, of shade trees and concrete jungles. After a bewildering series of left and right turns, Jack stopped in front of a bottle-strewn lot flanked by two faceless, soulless apartment buildings.

"That's where I grew up." His voice was flat, detached. "The building was condemned and razed while I was in jail. Ma and Katherine were kicked into public housing."

"Thank God for that," said Flynn, meaning it. "They could have been kicked out into the street."

"Might have been better off. Ma never found a way to handle the shame." He eased his foot down on the gas pedal and they moved away from the lot. "This place was falling apart before I was born. I couldn't wait to get the hell out of here. Ma used to say I was born with an attitude and walking papers."

She could still see him, all towering anger and pain, as he sat by her hospital bed and tried to bend the world to his will. Warrior and healer. The dark angel of ancient myth battling the twentieth century.

Gently she brushed a lock of dark hair from his forehead. "And yet you never really made the break, did you?"

He started, as if she had struck a raw nerve. "There's nothing here for me."

"Yes, there is." She sensed the truth of her words deep in her soul. "This is the place that made you the man you are. You'll always be tied to it."

"What about you, Flynn? What place calls to you?"

She shrugged. "I never stayed in one place long enough to call it home. My dad's career kept us moving. I've been in Manhattan for about seven years. I guess that qualifies for some kind of record for me." There was a place, however, a place where she retreated when the world was too much for her. That little cottage up in the Berkshires, away from reality.

No one else had ever been there with her. None of her friends even knew of its existence. It was her refuge, her solitary haven—the magical place she longed to share with Flanagan one day.

They drove around for a while. He pointed out the public school he'd attended as a kid. Its windows were broken now; screens hung crazily from the frames. The church where he'd been baptized and made his first communion. The streets and alleys where he'd learned how to fight.

She tried to imagine how different her life would have been if her uncle hadn't found her after the accident and Jack had spirited her away to the tiny cold-water flat he'd found. Would they have made a go of it or would life—*real* life, harsh and uncompromising—have destroyed the miracle they'd found together?

"I must have been a fool to think you could live here," he said, as if reading her mind. "All I knew was that I wanted to protect you, keep you safe—" He exhaled a long, slow breath that spoke of the years that had separated them. "It never would have worked, would it?"

She couldn't deny the truth. "I loved Billy," she said softly. "Sooner or later I would have remembered that fact." Mourning was a vital part of the healing process, and she doubted if Jack, young and angry and painfully uncertain, could have waited for her emotional scars to heal.

She looked at him and saw the boy he had been, and her heart ached for the time they had lost.

"Don't you see, Flanagan? That's what makes this whole thing so miraculous! God or fate or whatever name you want to put to it has brought us together again at exactly the right time." Her heart was free and so was his. They were still young and healthy and eager to embrace life. "This is our time, Flanagan. *Our time.*"

The silence in the car grew. It deepened; it threatened like storm clouds scudding overhead. And then in an instant the sun broke through, and Jack Flanagan, inveterate cynic, threw back his head and laughed with joy.

FLYNN MADE IT to the South Street Seaport on time the next morning for the fashion shoot. In fact, she was not only on time, she was rested, bright-eyed and incredibly happy.

And that happiness showed.

"Lookin' good," said Mac the stylist as he set up the wind machines. "What's his name?"

Flynn never had the chance to answer because Jenny, the photographer, beat her to the punch. "Don't you read the papers, Mac? The girl's got herself a new man."

Flynn gave what she hoped was a mysterious smile.

"Big picture of the two of them," Jenny continued, "walking into some fancy hotel on Paradise Island."

The stylist waggled his eyebrows. "Does he have a name?"

"Yes," said Flynn.

They waited a full minute. She felt no obligation to fill that silence.

"Wild Man Flanagan," said Jenny at last, "even if she refuses to tell you."

Mac staggered back in mock alarm. "The guy's dangerous."

Flynn looked at him calmly. "Really?"

Jenny laughed and fiddled with her light meter. "Always the cool one, aren't you, Flynn? The guy's hands are lethal weapons."

She shrugged. "I couldn't say. I haven't known him that long."

Jenny's voice took on an arch tone. "That's not what I've heard."

Flynn's breath caught. *Oh, please not that...* "There you go again, Jenny," she said, her voice light and breezy. "I warned you about getting your information from page six in the *New York Post*."

"Would you believe page one?"

Under the byline of one Donald Reid was a screaming tabloid-style headline proclaiming Flynn and Flanagan as star-crossed lovers who had found each other when Flanagan saved her life.

Or, as Reid had put it: "...after Wild Man Flanagan pulled Mary Scott Pennington from the burning wreckage of her wedding car..."

She tossed the paper to the ground.

"Come on, Flynn," said Jenny as she aimed her Hasselblad. "Give us some heat."

But it wasn't heat that the camera caught; it was fear.

Illogical. Irrational. But fear, nevertheless.

She turned and went to call Flanagan.

DONALD REID LOOKED into his bathroom mirror that morning and wished he had shades. The glare from his ear-to-ear grin was blinding.

"You did it," he said to his reflection. "You finally did it!"

His story on Wild Man and the president's little girl was splashed across the front page of the *Post* and twenty-five other dailies across the country. And that wasn't even the half of it. He'd concentrated on the romance and the other melodramatic elements that made for great tabloid journalism, but there was a hell of a lot more left to write on this story. He'd been one hundred percent on target. Thank God Flanagan had given his right name to the hospital staff all those years ago.

That was the key that had unlocked the rest. All these years he'd wondered about the true story behind Frederick Scott's death, dreamed about it, worried over it, and now he knew. It was all figured out, down to the last detail, and tucked away in a computer. This was bigger than Watergate, more frightening than either of the Kennedy assassinations.

For the first time in his life, he held all the cards, all the decks and all the chips.

Donahue and Oprah had called. Regis and Kathie Lee and Sally Jessy waited in the wings to catch him in his spare time.

"Spare time? Hah!" He shook his can of shaving cream and squirted a marshmallow glob of the stuff into the palm of his hand. He had an appointment in forty minutes to appear on two radio broadcasts across town. WNBC said the car would be waiting in front of the Manhattan hotel in fifteen minutes. No doubt about it: he was on his way up.

He'd ride out the glory train for the next few days, then as soon as his allotted fifteen minutes of fame began to dim, he would break the rest of the story, and the rest, as they say, would be history. His name would be on the lips of Donaldson and Jennings and Rather.

School kids would read about him in history books for the next hundred years. The sky was the limit.

He rummaged through the medicine cabinet for his Bic disposable. Pretty soon he'd be paying some guy to stop by the house with the hot scented towels and a finely honed straight-edge razor. He slathered the foam on his cheeks and chin. "Way to go, Reid," he mumbled.

He'd sent his wife out on a no-limit shopping spree. Maybe he'd find his kids some English nanny to change their Pampers and puree their strained peas.

He maneuvered the Bic along his left cheek. He heard the apartment door close.

"You're out of practice, baby," he called out to his wife. "Gotta learn to shop till you drop. We're heading into the big time."

Strange. She didn't laugh. The wife usually had a sense of humor in the worst of times. He hoped she wasn't going to turn out to be the kind of woman who didn't know how to relax and enjoy the fast lane.

"Come on in here and watch your Pulitzer prize-winning old man get ready for a date with live TV," he hollered.

She still didn't say anything but at least he heard her walking through the hallway toward the bathroom. Maybe he'd sell the house in Florida and buy a fancy place in the Dakota. "You gaining weight, babe?" She sounded like a linebacker with her shoes thudding against the floor like that.

He scrunched his mouth up to shave that little spot beneath his lower lip. "Whaddya think?" he asked as the door swung open. "Should I grow a beard or—"

"No time, Reid," said the man in the black mask. "You just ran out of time."

Chapter Eleven

Flynn's phone call pulled Jack out of a meeting with three of the top New York sportswriters. He listened quietly while she told him about the newspaper article but the significance eluded him. She was frantic about their earlier relationship not being made public, and when he questioned her about it, she simply said, "I don't know why, Flanagan. A feeling. I just wish this had never happened."

From nowhere jealousy sprang to life in his gut. White-hot flames of it. He wondered if she was thinking of her dead husband, wishing she were with him right now. If she had been with him, he would have made violent, passionate love to her, driving thoughts of all other men from her mind once and for all. He hated himself for the violence of his feelings, but he didn't deny them.

"Sorry," he said, taking his seat once again. "Where were we?"

The *New York Times* and *Newsday* reporters looked at each other. "The comparison between your style and Marciano's."

Jack knew they were speaking English, but the words somehow didn't connect. He couldn't get the frantic sound of Flynn's voice from his mind.

"Yeah," he said, wishing he still smoked. "Me and Marciano. Well, uh...I'd say..." *I wish we could run away, Flanagan. I don't want them to dredge up the accident....*

The reporter from the *Daily News* leaned forward. "Something wrong, champ?"

Jack shook his head, wishing he could shake away the prickle of apprehension between his shoulder blades. "Nothing major." He forced a laugh. "Now you see why Oscar makes as much dough as he does. He's the brains of this outfit."

"Where is he anyway?" asked the *News*. "Any problems?"

"Oscar got himself a bad case of fear of flying. He's taking Amtrak back." He gave them a brief, funny account of their unfunny emergency landing. He glanced at his watch. Where the hell *was* Oscar anyway? He could've walked back to New York by now. "He should be here any time now. He's the one to tell you about Marciano. He's the only one of us who remembers the guy."

The reporters spent a good few minutes trading stories about Oscar and his legendary training techniques. Oscar wasn't above scare tactics, most of which had worked wonders on the young Jack Flanagan.

"I'd still be in the slammer if it wasn't for Oscar," said Jack. "He was the first person to get it through my head that violence could be put to a better use." Jail had been a living hell. Day after day of empty, aching helplessness coupled with a rage that was out of control. Oscar had saved his life. Pulled Jack up by the ear and showed him the right path, and when Jack occasionally veered from the straight and narrow, it was Oscar who kicked his butt back on track. Oscar was friend and mentor, father and friend.

Jack usually didn't talk like that in front of reporters. He tended toward the monosyllabic and left the philosophizing for Oscar.

"Good stuff, Wild Man," said the guy from *Newsday*, as he slipped a brand-new tape into his machine. "Never knew you could wax poetic like this."

"Neither did I," said Jack. His emotions were right up-front today. He couldn't have hidden his feelings if his life depended on it. Love could be a dangerous commodity.

They talked a bit more about the current state of professional boxing and mob involvement, about the rise of different ethnic minorities, and then Jack saw his opening.

He popped open a can of beer and leaned back in his chair. "Hey, do any of you know a reporter named Reid?"

"Not personally," said the *News*, "but I sure as hell read the story in the morning edition. How true is it?"

"Can't answer that," said Jack, dragging a hand through his hair. "I haven't read it yet."

"Is it true you saved her life?" asked the *Times*.

"Yeah."

"And you're together now?" *Newsday* chimed in.

Jack hesitated. The urgency in Flynn's voice still echoed in his head but his need to stake his claim overrode his caution. "We're together."

One of the reporters whistled low. "Lucky man."

"You're right," said Jack. "A very lucky man."

"I met Reid a time or two," offered the *Times*. "Nice guy. Usually down on his luck if I remember right." The guy paused, tugging at his earlobe. "He wasn't always on the sports beat. Seems to me he had himself a major obsession with Frederick Scott's death back a few years when Reid was covering the national scene."

"Yeah," said the *News*. "I remember him now. Used to spend all his time in the library and on the phone. Got himself fired from three dailies because he couldn't let go."

Newsday cast a sharp look in Jack's direction. Jack did his best to keep his expression bland.

"Flynn is Scott's daughter, isn't she?"

"Guess so," said Jack as if it didn't matter. As if he didn't feel as though an army was walking over his grave.

But at least it makes sense, he thought after the reporters left. Reid had an ongoing interest in the Scott family. It figured Reid would be the one to put the pieces together.

There was nothing sinister in it, nothing suspicious. Their story would be front page news for a day or two and then would be pushed aside to make room for the latest hot gossip to hit town. Fifteen minutes of fame; that's all you get.

And it seemed to Jack they'd already had more than their allotted time.

He didn't mind the spotlight. His personal life had been spread all across the tabloids from the first day he stepped into the ring. Jail was a fact of his life; he wasn't ashamed that he'd been given a chance to learn from his youthful mistakes. There'd never been anything—or anyone—else worth protecting.

But it was different now. Now there was Flynn. Flynn who had her own painful past to contend with and who preferred to do so away from the glare of the media spotlight. As soon as she showed up at the apartment, he'd whisk her away to his cabin in upstate New York and stay there until the clamor died down.

She didn't want to think about the past, about the accident that took her husband. Neither did Jack. He wished he could drive all memory of her husband from her mind and make her his forever. Her husband was a shadow between them, a ghost he couldn't hear to see or touch but as real as the man once was. He could fight a man; he couldn't fight a memory.

Fate had thrown them together the first time, and it was fate that brought them back together now. In the normal scheme of things, their worlds would never have connected. They had no common frames of reference, no mutual friends, none of the normal things that bind a couple together. What they shared was passion.

For Jack it wasn't enough.

What he wanted from her was love. Love without shadows or ghosts or conditions.

The impossible kind.

THE MOMENT THE PHOTOGRAPHER had enough shots of Flynn, she slipped back into her jeans and T-shirt, grabbed her leather satchel and disappeared. She didn't even bother to remove the dramatic high fashion makeup. She'd had enough of the innuendo, the questions, the stage whispers. All she wanted was to get out of there and back into Flanagan's arms where nothing could hurt her.

Thirty minutes later she walked into the apartment. She tossed down her satchel, kicked off her flats and was about to call to Jack when he appeared in the living-room doorway.

"Flanagan?" He looked pale, haggard, drastically different from the man she had kissed goodbye a few hours earlier. "Are you all right?" Just a handful of days ago he had suffered brutal punishment at the hands of Killer Curtis. Dear God, please don't let there be anything wrong with him. He was so strong, so powerful—and she needed him so much.

"Oscar." His voice was raw with emotion. "He's—"

Flynn was at his side in an instant. "Dead?" Her own voice was a whisper.

Flanagan shook his head. "He's alive." His eyelids closed briefly. "In a hospital in Philly."

"I don't understand. We saw him board Amtrak in Delaware."

"Cops say the train ran into trouble around Philly and was held up there a few hours. Closest they can tell, Oscar went off with some woman who had a goon beat all hell out of him."

Flynn started to tremble uncontrollably and leaned against Flanagan for support. She could feel the electric hum of anger rippling through his body.

"How bad are his injuries?"

"Concussion, fractured right cheekbone, broken jaw."

"Poor Oscar." She started toward the telephone on the hall table. "I'll call for a car and we'll be in Philadelphia in a few hours."

"No, Flynn."

She turned, telephone in hand, and looked over at him. "Flying would probably take us longer, Jack. This is rush hour—we'd never make it to the airport before eight o'clock."

"I'm going by myself."

She punched in the number of the radio car company. "Absolutely not. I'm going with you."

He took the phone away from her and put it back in its cradle. "You're staying here."

"I'm a big girl, Flanagan. I go where I want to go."

"Not this time." He pulled her against him, capturing her hands behind her back in a gesture of pure male dominance. "I don't know exactly what happened to Oscar, Flynn. I'll be damned if I'm going to worry about you, too."

"Nobody's asking you to worry about me. I have the right to see Oscar."

His grip on her wrists tightened uncomfortably, and she became acutely aware of his strength.

"You're staying here." His mouth claimed hers, drawing her soul from her body with the intensity of his kiss.

She sagged against him. "I'm staying here." The breakneck pace of the past few days seemed to catch up with her all at once, and it required an act of will to stand upright.

"Be careful, Flanagan," she whispered as they said goodbye at the door. "I couldn't bear to lose you."

"You never will," he said. "I waited too long to find you again."

The door closed behind him, and Flynn choked on hot, painful sobs that started in her chest and tore their way up through her throat. *You're overreacting,* her brain cautioned. *Oscar will be fine. Flanagan will be back in less than twenty-four hours.* Jack was only driving to Philadelphia, not marching off to war. She was a mass of exposed nerve endings, exhausted and living at the outer edge of her emotions where joy could easily turn to sorrow.

Jack had exploded into her life, shattering her ideas of what her future would hold. The past few days had brought little sleep, although there were some wonderful forms of compensation. Add to that their near-miss on the private jet, the unwanted publicity and Oscar's accident—was it any wonder she felt shell-shocked?

Maybe that would explain the twinge of guilt stabbing her just beneath the rib cage. *He's as vulnerable as you are. Don't keep taking from him if you have nothing to give in return.*

Billy had been in her thoughts a great deal the past few days. Years ago she had struggled with tremendous guilt that she had lived and he had not. The doctor in Switzerland had said that was a normal part of grieving, that it was natural for the one left behind to feel guilty at his or her own good fortune.

Flynn hadn't even tried to explain that that wasn't the type of guilt she was feeling. Her guilt went deeper and was much harder to put into words. She felt responsible for Billy's death, as if the simple act of loving her had somehow sealed his fate. He had been there in her life for as long as she could remember, one of a series of strong male figures to whom she could turn for love and for safety. She had been protected from girlhood on, first by her father, then by Billy, then by her Uncle Hugh. Now Flanagan had stepped into her life to keep her safe from harm.

She loved her father and then she lost him. She had loved her late husband, too. Guilt seemed an intrinsic part of the equation.

"Ridiculous!" she said aloud to the empty room. Even more ridiculous that she felt the same way now— but this time about Jack. And coupled with her incongruous sense of guilt was the knowledge that the act of loving wasn't always enough to create a happy ending. Loving Billy had been as easy as breathing; indeed, she had loved him almost from the time she took her first step. It had been Billy who held her hand during those terrible days after her father's sudden death, Billy who made the world seem less dark and frightening. Billy who had made her feel less alone.

Now there was Jack to keep her safe. There was nothing wrong with that. Women turned toward men for physical protection. They always had and they always would. But why then did that make her feel guilty, as if she took and took from him and offered him nothing in return? If the tables were turned, would she be able to offer him the unconditional love he gave to her so freely? Would she—

"I'm tired," she said aloud. "That's all this is."

Her mind was playing tricks on her out of sheer exhaustion.

A good night's sleep would make all the difference in the world.

HUGH SCOTT'S JET LANDED at JFK a few minutes after nine p.m. The pilot brought the plane to a stop a few hundred feet from a small private terminal at the outskirts of the airport and, seconds later, Thomas Judd boarded.

"Judd." Hugh Scott inclined his head and continued his painstaking reading of a military brief.

"Perfect," said Judd, sitting down on the arm of the chair before Scott. "All went like clockwork. I had—"

Scott raised one hand. "Later."

"But—"

"Later."

Damn fool. Judd had been in the business long enough to know you did not talk in front of nonclassified personnel. The two men waited until the plane had emptied of flight crew, pilots and mechanics.

"It's done?" Scott dropped his paperwork into a leather briefcase and locked it.

"Completely. Perfectly. Without a trace."

"No more stories digging up the past?"

Judd laughed. "Only if another reporter picks up the torch."

Scott, to his surprise, joined in the laughter. "Then we merely replay the scene, do we not?"

"As often as necessary."

"And the pugilist? You've put the plan in motion."

"Don't worry, boss," said Judd. "His days are numbered."

OSCAR MAY HAVE BEEN BLOODIED, but he was definitely unbowed. Unfortunately that fact wasn't enough to erase the enormous guilt Jack battled with as he sat by his friend's hospital bed at the U of P later that evening.

"After all these years telling you to keep your guard up, look what happened to me." Oscar battled with a smile. "You'd think I was some marshmallow right off the street."

Jack couldn't manage an answering smile. "What the hell happened?" he demanded. "Who did this to you?"

"Would you believe a woman?"

"Try again."

"I'm tellin' you the truth, boy. I met up with this lady while we were waiting for the train to get repaired, and next thing I know, I'm in a Philly hospital."

"I think you're leaving a few things out of this story, Oscar."

"We went out to dinner. So help me, Johnny, the last thing I remember is digging into an antipasto then a—"

"You telling me a woman beat hell out of you?"

Oscar considered that for a moment. "No, but I am tellin' you she's got herself one good scam going. Took my wallet and credit cards and my Rolex. I'd love to meet up with the bozo she works with and—"

A nurse came in, adjusted the painkiller dripping into Oscar's vein, then disappeared.

"There's more," said Oscar, his smile fading.

Jack's adrenaline surged. "It's about me?"

"'Fraid so. Add up the clues, Johnny. Did you ever think this might be the mob's way of saying hi? Out on the street they're sayin' you owe them one fight."

"I'm retired."

"Boxers have been known to change their minds."

"Not me. I'm getting on with my life."

"You're the only one who kept his nose clean, Johnny. They don't like that."

"Tough," said Flanagan. "They'll just have to learn to live with it."

"Flynn's a good kid and I like her a lot, but the timing just isn't right, Johnny. Something's brewing out there. I can almost smell it. Give her up before someone gets hurt. All these years they tried to get under your skin—well, now they finally have something they can use to get to you. This is just the start. Let them find your Achilles' heel and you're done for. Use your head, boy, not your—"

"It's too late," said Jack, staring out the window at the setting sun. "Giving her up's the one thing I can't do."

"Then God help you," said Oscar, "because I got a feeling there's some rough times ahead."

IN NEW YORK CITY that evening, the O'Neals were entertaining their best friends.

"The baby looks absolutely adorable," said Holland Chambers, chucking her godchild under the chin, "but you, my dear, look like hell."

"Thanks so much." Joanna thanked God for the dim lighting in the tiny den. Perhaps inviting their friends to dinner had been a mistake.

"Now out with it, Joanna. What's wrong? Motherhood? Marriage? Mid-life crises?"

"All of the above," said Joanna. "None of the above. Oh God, I wish I could tell you."

Holland slumped back in her chair. From the living room came the low deep sounds of Ryder and Alistair in conversation. "PAX again. Why didn't I guess?"

"It's Ryder," said Joanna, lowering her voice. "He's obsessed."

"Don't complain, honey. It puts a bloom in a girl's cheeks."

Joanna gestured impatiently. "I'm not talking about sex."

"Somehow I didn't think so. A case he's working on?"

Joanna hesitated. She would give anything to be able to tell her best friend everything, but she had to forego that luxury for a necessary lie. "He's out of the field now, Holland. He'll be working strictly on technical problems from here on out."

"The gentleman farmer from Connecticut?"

"If we get there in one piece."

Holland leaned forward. "What, exactly, is he obsessed with?"

"An idea." She shook her head as if to clear it. "Not even an idea, a memory. A feeling." She briefly sketched a few of Ryder's less inflammatory suspicions about the death of Frederick Scott almost fifteen years ago. "He's convinced Frederick Scott's daughter is in danger."

"I saw those photos of her with that big, gorgeous prizefighter. That kind of danger a woman doesn't mind."

"Don't make jokes. I'm terrified." Ryder had been out of control these past few days. Their apartment was littered with clippings dating back to 1974. He'd spent hours at the computer, tapping into data bases around the world, searching for the one clue that would lead him to the answer. "He wants to go back undercover and nail Scott."

"For doing what? The 'crime' only exists in his mind."

"Try telling Ryder that. We're so close, Holland, so darned close to getting out of this safely, and he's willing to throw it all away because he hates Hugh Scott."

"Hugh Scott?" Holland's elegant brows lifted. "Matinee idol material. That man is definitely in the wrong line of work." She looked hard at Joanna who was having a terrible time dissembling. "Nobody hates Hugh Scott."

Joanna shrugged, as if at a loss for words. She'd already gone too far. "Just pray your husband can convince my husband of that." She buried her face against her daughter's chubby neck. *This is what's important, Ryder. Why can't you see that?*

AND THAT'S EXACTLY what she told him two hours later when they were alone.

"I can't believe you did such a damned stupid thing," Ryder raged. "Are you trying to sabotage this case on me?"

"Absolutely not!" she raged back. "What I'm trying to do is make you understand what you owe to us."

He grabbed her by the shoulders. "I love you, Jo. I love our daughter. I know exactly what I owe to both of you."

She pulled away from him. "If you really did, you wouldn't be doing this."

"It's because I love you that I have to do this."

Her laughter teetered on the edge of hysteria. "Try again, Ryder. I won't buy that excuse."

"Knowing what I know, if I let this thing go I'm no better than the bastards who killed Frederick Scott."

"Let it rest, Ryder." She was implacable in her fear. "You don't have to save the world."

"I don't want to save the world. I want to save one part of it."

Damn the tears that filled her eyes. "And I want to save you."

"Just give me some time, Jo. I know this is going to come to a head any day now. I can feel it—"

"Stop this, Ryder! My God, you've gone mad. Don't you realize no one believes you? Not even Alistair understands what on earth you're talking about."

"I don't give a damn if the whole world thinks I'm nuts. Just work with me, Jo. I'm right. I know I'm right."

She swallowed around the painful lump in her throat. "I'm asking you not to go."

His look tore at her heart. "And I'm asking you to understand."

"I can't," she said, her voice low and defeated. "I just can't." Living on the edge was fine when you were responsible for no one but yourself. Living on the edge when you were the parent of an infant was irresponsible.

She went into the bedroom to pack her bags.

Chapter Twelve

Flynn was glad she had no appointments the next day because after Jack called and told her Oscar would be just fine, sleep still eluded her. She tossed and turned until daybreak then dragged herself out of bed to watch the crack-of-dawn news shows that had become popular. The hard news show led into the softer *Good Morning America*, and she stumbled into the kitchen to make some coffee. Unfortunately she caught a glimpse of herself in the shiny side of the toaster oven. Huge dark circles ringed her eyes. The dark circles could be camouflaged by skillful makeup, but there was no camouflage available for the look of fear.

"Oscar's fine," she said aloud as she filled the Mr. Coffee with bottled water. "Jack is on his way home. I have nothing to worry about."

She puttered around the kitchen, making herself a scrambled egg and toast while the coffee made itself, then carried everything back to the living room in time for more news.

"Sorry, George," she said as a picture of the president flashed onto the screen. "I'm getting very tired of this kinder, gentler world." She put down the tray of food and reached for the remote control. Her finger was poised on the button, ready to defect to the *Today* show when a familiar face looked out at her.

"Uncle Hugh!" She sat down on the edge of her chair. The last she'd heard, her uncle was still in Geneva, toiling away on the endless work surrounding the latest disarmament package. Any time he was in the United States, he made it a point of ringing her up for dinner. Strange he would be in New York on ". . . personal business . . ." and not contact her.

She sat there, staring at the screen, as it faded into the next story. Uncle Hugh probably figured she was still in the Caribbean or somewhere else on a photo shoot. Her answering machine had been in the shop for three weeks now, and she still hadn't gotten around to hiring a service for the interim. Short of sending a telegram or ferreting out her invisible agent, there was no way he could have contacted her.

But there was nothing to stop her from contacting him, was there?

So what if he and Jack had had their problems years ago. Her uncle probably didn't even remember the incident and, if he did, surely he would never connect it with the Jack Flanagan of today. Maybe it was time for her to bring her two favorite men together.

She reached for the cordless phone on the end table and punched in her uncle's New York number.

"Hugh Scott speaking."

"Uncle Hugh! It's Flynn. Welcome home."

A beat pause then, "Mary Flynn. Darling! I was going to ring you up after breakfast." His baritone chuckle reminded her so much of her father.

She swallowed hard against her memories. "It's so wonderful to hear your voice."

"It's been too long, hasn't it? When are you going to fly over to Geneva for that nice long vacation you've been talking about for ages now?"

She took a deep breath. "That's one of the reasons I called, Uncle Hugh. I'd love to stop by and bring someone along to meet you."

"A new boyfriend?"

It was her turn to pause. "Actually he's more than a boyfriend. His name is Jack Flanagan, he's the heavyweight champion of the world, and I think I'm in love." *Coward, Mary Flynn. You know you're in love with him.*

"I know," said her uncle. "I saw the photographs in the morning paper." His voice lowered with concern. "How long has this been going on?"

"Not very." This certainly wasn't the time to talk about second chances and destiny. The past was bound to be a sore spot between the two men; better to table it for as long as possible. "I want my two favorite men to meet," she said, sounding cheerful and unconcerned. "Are you free for dinner tonight?"

"Darling, you know I'd love nothing better than to get together with you and your young man—Flanagan, is it?—but I'm flying back to Geneva later this afternoon."

She didn't know whether to be disappointed or relieved. "Short visit, wasn't it?"

"You know government service, Mary Flynn. Unpredictable, to say the least." He chatted a few minutes about some acquaintances they had in common, and she told him all about the prize fight in Nassau and the bumpy plane ride home. "Just like your father," he mused. "Frederick hated flying until the day he died."

"You miss him, don't you?" His words surprised Flynn. Hugh Scott rarely spoke of the beloved brother who had died too young.

"Let's not dwell on sorrow," her uncle said, ever the diplomat. "Let's plan for you and your young man to join me for dinner the next time I'm in the States."

"Take care of yourself," said Flynn. "Remember: you're the only family I have left."

"I know," said Hugh Scott. "That's one thing I never forget."

Flynn hung up the telephone. How wonderful it had been to hear her uncle's voice. Jack was wrong to worry abut how they would get along. Hugh Scott didn't seem to associate the adult Jack Flanagan with the boy who had trashed the nurses' station ten years ago. Certainly when her uncle found out, both he and Jack would find a way to let the past remain exactly that: the past.

She puttered about the apartment for a few minutes, one eye on the clock and the other on the television. What she should do was eat breakfast, polish off the rest of the coffee and watch the news again on the hour. Maybe by then Jack would be home and she would be in his arms, and this odd feeling of impending doom would vanish once and for all.

She didn't have long to wait. The doorbell chimed. "Jack!" She leaped to her feet, overturning the lap tray, and ran to the door.

"Flynn Pennington?"

She frowned at the man with the spiky hair who stood at her front door. "If you're a reporter, you can—"

"I'm not a reporter." He handed her a pile of ID cards through the narrow door opening.

She examined the stack of cards. "The government? I'm certain my taxes are up-to-date."

"This isn't about your income taxes. I'd like to talk to you."

"I'll give you the number of my agency. You can call and make an appointment."

His smile was gentle, almost sad. That frightened her more than outright aggression. "I'm afraid this is a personal issue."

"Mr.—" She looked down at the top card. "Mr. O'Neal, I think we should postpone this until this afternoon. I had a poor night's sleep and I—"

"This is a highly sensitive topic, Mary Flynn."

Mary Flynn. She stared at him. "Do I know you?"

"In a way. I worked for your uncle years ago."

Dear God, don't look at me like that. . . . She chose to deliberately misunderstand. "I'm sorry if you had difficulties with Uncle Hugh, but I don't see how I can help you."

"You can't," said O'Neal, "but if you listen to me, maybe you can help Jack Flanagan."

THE TAXI LET JACK OFF in front of Flynn's apartment building a few minutes before noon. Oscar had been transferred to a hospital in Boston near his sister. Jack had seen his friend safely on his way, then flagged down a cab to take him to Flynn's.

Being away from her had been a living hell. The touch and sight and smell of her was etched in his brain for all time. Twenty-four hours had seemed a lifetime. Only concern for her safety had prompted him to leave her behind.

Never again, he vowed as he strode up the sidewalk to her front door. Not for a day or an hour or a minute. He stopped just shy of the doorway and turned to look over his shoulder. A man, a few inches shorter than he and with spiky brown hair, stood partially obscured by a planter.

Damn reporters. Didn't they ever give up?

Jack entered the building.

"FLYNN? I'm back."

Flynn's heart pounded at the sound of Flanagan's voice in the hallway as he made his way toward her bedroom. More than anything she wanted to turn to him and hold him close, but that option was no longer hers. *Run. You have to run.* Swallowing hard, she continued to pack her suitcase.

A pair of strong arms slipped around her waist. "Here you are." He kissed the side of her neck, and she found herself blinking away tears.

She moved out of his arms and toward the dresser across the room where she carefully selected a few silky teddies in sherbet colors, then draped them over her arm. "How is Oscar?"

"Back in Boston where he belongs. His sister will be looking out for him until he's back on his feet." Her heart ached over what she had to do.

She met his eyes for the first time and noted how tired and vulnerable he looked. *Dear God, if there were any other way...*

He stepped between her and her suitcase. "Going someplace?"

"As a matter of fact, I am." She tossed the lingerie into her suitcase, painfully aware of his scrutiny. "An old friend invited me to a yachting party off Montauk Point."

He nodded, arms crossed over his powerful chest. "Can you bring a new friend?"

Flanagan was a proud man. How much that question must have cost him. *The choice is yours,* O'Neal had said. *It's all up to you....* But, of course, there was no choice at all. Not really. O'Neal's words were a jumble of bits and pieces tumbling around inside her brain. Accidents that were no accidents at all. "Get out!" she had screamed at O'Neal. "I don't want to hear this!" But he kept talking, saying terrible, frightening things, even as she dialed for the security force. All of it—everything—pointed toward the fact that if Jack was to live, she would have to give him up. She didn't need to hear everything O'Neal had to say. By the time the apartment building security reached her front door, she had heard all she needed to know; still, the sense that there was more—much more—lingered.

One thing, however, was certain: nothing mattered more than keeping Jack safe.

"I said, how about bringing a new friend with you?"

"I'd really love to, Flanagan, but the guest list isn't up to me."

A muscle in his jaw twitched dangerously. "Maybe you should skip this party."

"Wish I could, but it's too important." She flashed him a brittle, professional smile. "Business, you know."

"How long you planning to be gone."

"A few days."

"If this is a payback for leaving you yesterday, I get the message."

"I don't know what you're talking about, Jack." She busied herself with arranging the teddies in the suitcase. *I have to go, Jack. I have to leave you as fast as I can run. Don't make this any harder than it already is....* "This was a spur of the moment invitation from an old friend. Nothing more."

The tension in the room increased.

"Who's the friend?"

"You've never met."

"Right." He stepped closer. "We don't exactly run in the same circles, do we, Flynn?"

She closed the lid on her suitcase and calmly began packing cosmetics in a small travel kit. "Don't you think you're overreacting?"

"Level with me. Give me a name."

She prayed for the courage to see this through. She owed him this much and more. "Frank Baldwin." It was the name of a soap opera star she'd met at a party and disliked on sight. She continued sorting through vials and jars of makeup.

Suddenly the makeup jars went flying across the room, and she found her wrists captured in his powerful grip. "Who is this guy?"

"I told you. An old friend."

"Boyfriend?"

"That's an antiquated term."

"I'll give you till the count of three to give me a straight answer."

I love you, Flanagan. If I could only make you understand that's why I'm doing this.... "Yes, Jack. An old boyfriend."

He stared at her for what seemed the longest moment of her life then released her hands as if the mere touch of her skin disgusted him.

You gave my life back to me, Jack ... it's the least I can do for you ...

"Stop looking at me like that." She struggled to keep her tone airy and unconcerned. "We don't own each other, do we? It's only for a few days, Jack. I'll be back before you know it."

"All or nothing, Flynn. I already told you I won't share you with any man."

"I understand."

"And you're still going on that boat?"

"I'm still going."

The muscle in his jaw worked furiously; she longed to reach up and touch his cheek just one last time. The temptation was too much to bear, and she raised her hand and brought it up to his face. *Just once more and I'll never ask for anything else....*

"Don't." The word vibrated with his rage. "Whatever you do, don't touch me."

"Jack, I—"

His cry was primitive, savage in its intensity. Flynn didn't cower or move away. She knew he could kill her in the blink of an eye if he wanted to. She also knew he would never hurt her.

He grabbed the desk chair, and Flynn watched, terrified, as he sent it hurtling toward the French doors.

"Goodbye, Flynn," he said over the shriek of shattering glass. "It's been fun." Then he turned and walked out of her life.

She was proud of herself. He never did see her cry.

And he never heard her whisper, "I love you."

JACK WANTED TO DRIVE his fist through the steel doors of the elevator. He wanted to hear the sound of bone cracking, see the arc of blood, feel the hot white pain spread through his body.

He wanted anything that would drive away the yawning blackness sweeping over him, pulling him down deep into despair.

The saddest thing was that he'd really believed that he and Flynn were in it for the long haul, that what they had together had "forever" stamped all over it.

He'd believed it until he saw her packing her bag, and telling him that going from his bed to the arms of another man was nothing out of the ordinary.

Maybe in her world it wasn't.

He stormed out of the elevator and passed an old lady with a string shopping bag who shrank away from him in fear. He tore through the lobby and pushed open the door, nearly knocking the liveried doorman to the ground.

The hot wet air of a New York summer slapped him in the face. He kept walking. Visions of Flynn's long legs wrapped around the back of another man rose up from the sunbaked sidewalk. He kept walking. The sound of her cries of passion as another man touched her filled his brain. He kept walking. Her smell, her taste—

The look in her eyes when she told him to go.

He stopped walking.

He closed his eyes and replayed the scene in her bedroom minutes ago. *We don't own each other, do we?* Her voice surrounded him. He recalled nuance and intonation, all of which told him he was wasting his time. But the look in her eyes told him something different. Her beautiful eyes had told him to stay.

FLYNN COULDN'T stop trembling.

Despite the hot, humid air streaming through the shattered French doors, she was cold right down to her bones. *You did what you had to do.* Although she wasn't entirely convinced that what Ryder O'Neal had told her was true, she couldn't take a chance with Flanagan's life. O'Neal's identification was impressive, she'd grant him that, and he knew enough arcane detail about her uncle's appointment to the Court of St. James's to give her pause.

Only the thought of losing Flanagan forever the way she'd lost Billy made it possible for those treacherous lies to pass her lips so easily. She closed her eyes, and tears burned her lids. She could live with a broken heart; what she couldn't live with was the knowledge that a man like Flanagan died because she'd been too selfish to act.

But, dear God, how dark and empty her life looked without him by her side. Without his arms to hold her. Without the chance to build a future and raise a family and grow old next to him.

Her father used to hum an old song that claimed love was lovelier the second time around. She laughed hollowly and looked down at the street. More painful. More frightening. More fragile. But lovelier? She doubted if she would have chosen that word to describe the emotions at war inside her heart.

The front doorbell buzzed.

"Go away," she whispered. The last thing she wanted was to be forced to make polite conversation with anyone.

The doorbell buzzed again. No Express Mail deliveries. No packages from UPS. No friendly chatter with the friendly divorcée next door.

Silence. She waited. The doorbell didn't buzz again. Instead, the door itself flew open, and Flanagan stormed into the hallway.

He'd probably come to kill her.

She didn't know whether to laugh or cry or run. So she stood her ground.

"Lay one hand on me, Flanagan, and I'll scream this apartment house down around your ears."

He said nothing, just moved toward her.

"I'm not joking, Flanagan." She must be crazy. Hope began to bubble up from deep inside. "If I don't show up at the yacht, they'll know something happened."

Still he moved toward her.

A smarter woman might have moved away. "Flanagan, take one more step and I'll—" Too late. She was in his arms, his mouth on hers, swept away on a tide of joy greater than anything she'd ever imagined.

"You're not going anywhere," he said.

"I have to."

He stole her breath with a passionate, earthshaking kiss. "I'm not going to let you."

Dear God, how beautiful he was.... "You can't stop me. I have a life of my own, Jack."

"Not anymore. We're in this together."

"Go away," she said, her voice breaking. "I'm no good for you, Jack. Find someone else."

"There is no one else." He held her close. "From that first moment, there's been no one but you."

O'Neal's words about danger and death and crazy, convoluted plots all but drowned out the sound of Jack's voice. She blinked. "What did you say?"

"I said we're in this together. There's no yacht trip, is there?"

She might as well go for broke. "A man came to see me. Ryder O'Neal. He used to work with my uncle."

"What did he want?"

"I—I don't know how to put this—"

"He's trying to split us up."

"Yes." Her voice was a whisper. "But not the way you think. He says you're in danger. He says—" She stopped. The idea was absurd, totally absurd. Why on earth was she lending it any credibility? "He says someone wants you dead." She told him all she remembered about O'Neal's conversation, stumbling over the accidents that had been anything but.

"The Mob," said Flanagan, dragging his hand through his hair. "Oscar warned me about them last night. Those sons of—"

"Not the Mob."

They spun around to see Ryder O'Neal standing in the archway to the bedroom.

"Who the hell are you?" Flanagan stepped forward, six and a half feet of menace.

Flynn placed her hand on his forearm. "That's Ryder O'Neal, Jack. He—"

Jack brushed her hand away and advanced on O'Neal. "If you're one of the goons who roughed up Oscar, I swear to God you won't make it out of this room in one piece."

"Like I told you before, it's not the Mob you have to worry about," said O'Neal. "It's her uncle."

JACK LISTENED to O'Neal's story without saying a word. O'Neal told it simply and without emotion, but the impact was like a sledge to Flynn's heart.

"I don't want to hear this." Flynn pushed Ryder aside and ran toward the living room. "You're lying. My uncle wouldn't—" She couldn't even say those words. What kind of man was Ryder O'Neal to make up such heinous lies? Her father. Secretary of State

Pennington. Her own Billy. And now Flanagan? "You're mad!" she screamed at O'Neal as he and Jack followed her into the room. "Tell him, Flanagan! Tell him he's wrong."

Jack looked at her, his dark eyes sorrowful, and still he said nothing.

O'Neal opened up a portfolio and handed her a sheaf of papers and photos. "I didn't want to have to show you these, but under the circumstances..."

O'Neal had spared her the autopsy photographs but little else. She read swiftly, her mind taking in the facts and figures and trying desperately to keep emotion at bay. "My father didn't die," she said at last. "He was murdered."

He glanced over at Flanagan who maintained his imposing silence. "President Scott got too close to uncovering a scheme your uncle was involved in. Senator Pennington came too close to uncovering the truth about your dad's death."

"My God..." Flynn's eyes filled with tears. "And Billy—?"

"Billy was carrying on his father's investigation."

"So he had to die."

O'Neal nodded. "He had to die."

Rage and sorrow battled inside her breast. "Why is Jack in danger?"

O'Neal explained that Hugh Scott's original plan, ten years ago, had included her own death. "He couldn't be sure you didn't know what Billy was up to. He couldn't take that chance." But a twist of fate in the form of Jack Flanagan had saved Flynn's life. "Somewhere along the way your uncle had a change of heart," O'Neal went on. "Your memory seemed spotty, at best. During those first months in Switzerland after the accident, he monitored your every waking moment. Your sessions with the doctors and the therapists were taped and transcribed. As time went on, he grew more certain you knew nothing about the Penningtons' investigation into your father's death." He shook his head sadly. "And there's the unbelievable fact that your uncle has come to care about you."

"Right," said Flanagan, breaking his silence. "And that's why he murdered her husband."

O'Neal rose and paced the living room as he continued his story. Both Flynn and her uncle had spent the past ten years putting the past from their minds. Then along came that same past in the form of Jack Flanagan, sweeping into Flynn's life once again and providing the bridge between what was and what would be.

"Jack is the one variable your uncle had never factored in," said O'Neal, taking his seat again. Hugh Scott wasn't about to take the chance that Flanagan would trigger Flynn's memory. "Donald Reid saw the connection and we all know what happened to him."

"Reid?" Jack's voice betrayed his surprise. "Reporter from Florida?"

"That's the one," said O'Neal.

Flynn swallowed. "What happened to him?"

"Dead," said O'Neal flatly. "Murdered in a hotel bathroom right after he broke the story about you and Flanagan."

Flynn looked out the window and down on the street below. A kaleidoscopic play of memories danced across her line of vision. Her father laughing at a press conference. Secretary Pennington's devotion to duty. The way Billy planned to continue his father's work. "I never knew," she whispered against the pane of glass. "Billy never said a word..." *A waste,* she thought. *A terrible, pathetic waste.*

"And you're telling me she's safe?" Jack asked. "How the hell can we believe Flynn isn't the next target?"

Flynn turned away from the window at Jack's words. His tone bristled with outrage, most of which seemed directed toward O'Neal.

"Scott has invested a great deal in his niece," O'Neal said, putting some distance between himself and Jack. "You have to remember Flynn is the last of the Scotts."

"You've done a lot of talking, O'Neal." Jack rose and approached the older—and smaller—man. "But you still haven't told us what you're going to do to fix things."

O'Neal didn't flinch under Jack's threatening scrutiny. "I'm going to need your help."

"What about that organization you're with?" Flynn asked. "Why can't they just take the information you've shown us and do something with it?"

O'Neal went through a convoluted explanation about the methods used to obtain evidence, but what it all boiled down to was a lack of support on the part of his superiors.

"You'll just have to trust me."

Flynn's laugh was harsh. "Trust you? Like I trusted my Uncle Hugh?"

"Mary, I—"

She raised a hand to stop O'Neal. "Don't say another word. I need time to think." The world looked crazier than it ever had. She needed to step back and consider it from every angle.

"We don't have time," said O'Neal.

"You're asking too much of me." She looked over at Jack. "Of us."

"Maybe I haven't made the situation clear enough," said O'Neal. "Two weeks is all you have, Mary. The hit on Jack will be made sometime between now and the twenty-fifth of June in a public place." The dates her uncle would be busily occupied preparing for another summit in Geneva.

"To look like a mob hit?" asked Jack.

O'Neal nodded. "Exactly. We can do our best to protect you, but you'll still have to be on the front line if we're going to trap Scott's men in the act."

"What about Flynn?"

They were talking about her as if she weren't even in the room.

"We can send her to a safe house until it's over."

"Okay." Flanagan extended his hand. "I'm in."

O'Neal rose and the two men shook on it. Flynn stared at them in amazement.

She rose and faced them. "May I ask what in hell you two are doing?"

They looked at her blankly.

"You'll send me to a safe house? How dare you."

Flanagan went to drape an arm around her shoulder but she pulled away. "It's for your own good, Flynn. We'll hire the finest security guards available.

Two weeks and then we'll have the rest of our lives to spend together."

"No."

He glowered at her. "No?"

"You heard me, Flanagan. No one is sending me away."

Flanagan's temper was rising but she didn't care. So was her own.

"If you think I'm going to risk your life, Flynn, you're crazy."

"And if you think I'm going to sit back and watch you risk your own, then you don't know me at all."

O'Neal headed toward the apartment door. "I think I'll wait outside." Neither Flynn nor Jack tried to stop him.

"You're being pigheaded," said Flanagan as the door closed after O'Neal.

"Equal partners, Flanagan," she said, heart hammering against her rib cage. "You can't protect me from everything."

"Yes, I can." His tone was fierce, almost angry. "No one will ever hurt you. I promise you that."

"Do you really think you can hide me away somewhere like a pretty little painted doll, then bring me back out when the trouble's over? I'm not a child any longer, Flanagan. My dad looked out for me. Then Billy." Her voice faltered for a moment. "Then my Uncle Hugh. You can see where that got me."

"I'm not like any of them. I'm not going to leave you, Flynn."

"Can you guarantee that?"

He hesitated.

"I don't think so. We're either in this together or it's over."

"Is that an ultimatum?"

She lifted her chin. "Yes." If they were going to have a future together, they would first have to deal with the past. She was through running from it.

They stood there, eyes locked, for what seemed hours.

"Together," said Jack, opening his arms to her. "All the way."

Chapter Thirteen

They believed him.

Ryder dodged a taxicab as he crossed Park at 57th Street. It had been a close call, but they believed him.

And, more importantly, they were going to play the game his way.

Flynn and Jack had kept him cooling his heels in the lobby for almost an hour. He'd bummed a cigarette from the doorman and paced a hole in the marble floor while he waited. When they'd called him upstairs, he'd pushed, prodded, and cajoled and was about to drop to his knees and beg when Flanagan said they would do whatever had to be done to bring Scott to justice. Unfortunately Ryder hadn't counted on Mary's unexpected reaction. Truth was, the girl Mary Scott was gone and a woman named Flynn had taken her place. She was her father's daughter, after all: strong and brave and loyal.

Flanagan was a lucky man.

He didn't blame them for having trouble believing the story. For a long time he'd had trouble with it himself.

Hugh Scott had once been an active, upright member of PAX, as Alistair had said. He was admired, respected, honored for his tireless efforts. But when his younger brother Frederick began moving up the political ladder, something in Hugh gave way and jealousy took over. Frederick was charming, brilliant, effortless in his decision-making. Always right. Always loved. Always all the things Hugh Scott struggled hard to be.

When Hugh got himself into a minor scrape while at the Court of St. James's, it was his brother the president who stood up for him. Instead of gratitude, Hugh felt rage. PAX didn't abandon him, but the opportunities to serve grew more infrequent until they dried up altogether, and he had to face the ugly fact that he had gone as far as he could within the company. Public opinion wanted him pulled from London. His brother ignored it.

Was it any wonder Hugh Scott had accepted the offer when it came in? Information for prestige. Information for money. Information for revenge.

It could have gone on like that forever.

But his brother Frederick had to push too far. Dig too deeply. Look too closely at matters most presidents would have brushed aside.

He had to die. There was no other way. An injection near the base of the skull. The illusion of a fatal stroke. He'd had the records sealed, the body cremated, the evidence destroyed.

The perfect crime.

Almost.

Now it was up to Ryder to make certain Flynn and Jack had a chance to make a life together—and that Hugh Scott paid the piper.

He had to take one last stab at getting Alistair on his side. His friend might be retired from PAX, but the Englishman still wielded a great deal of clout. One word from him, and Ryder would have all the help he needed to keep both Jack and Flynn as safe as possible.

Unfortunately the Chamberses weren't home. "Damn it," he breathed as he headed back out onto the street. Time was running out. If he didn't line up help and fast, those two kids wouldn't stand a chance in hell.

Flanagan's last words to him lingered in his ears. The fighter had followed Ryder out to the elevator. Instead of a polite goodbye, he had a warning: "Listen, you son of a bitch," Flanagan said. "If you want to risk your wife and kid's future playing James Bond, that's your business, but let one thing happen to the woman I love and I'll follow you to hell and back."

Ryder wandered into a Greek restaurant near Lexington Avenue. Flanagan's words burned at his gut. The expression in Flynn's eyes haunted him. He couldn't remember a time when he felt more helpless or more alone.

It was a little after midnight when he dragged himself back to the apartment. He inserted the key in the first lock. Joanna and the baby were probably up in the Connecticut house, sitting on the wraparound porch and looking up at the starry summer sky. He could have been there with them if only—

"No use thinking about it," he said as he pushed open the door. His decision had been made for him ten years ago on that street corner. He'd never forget the look in Flanagan's eyes as the boy sat in that police car and waited for the traffic light to change. Ryder knew all about the way Flanagan had felt that night; Ryder had been feeling that way since the day he figured out the truth about Hugh Scott.

He unbuttoned his shirt and sloughed it off. It fell to the floor unnoticed. He unhooked his belt. It lay coiled at the archway to the living room. He was about to unzip his trousers when he heard a loud and disgusted sigh.

"Don't tell me I have to civilize you all over again, Ryder."

He stopped, hands on the closure of his trousers. He wanted to believe but found it almost impossible to think he could be so lucky.

"Jo?"

Her soft laugh filled the darkened room. "Were you expecting someone else?"

From the nursery monitor came the hushed sweet sounds of his daughter's breathing. He thought his heart would burst through his chest from the rush of love and relief he felt at that moment.

"You're back?" Stupid words but the best he could do.

"I'm back."

"To stay?"

Again that laugh. "We made it as far as New Milford. You're a difficult habit to break, Ryder."

He knew what she wanted to hear. He wished with all his heart and soul that he could say it. "Nothing's changed, Jo." Sweat rolled down his back. "I still have to do it."

"Everything's changed," said the woman he loved. "God forgive me, but I've come back to help you."

LIVING ON THE EDGE proved to be more difficult than Flynn had anticipated. It was one thing to know the man you loved was in danger; it was quite another thing to step out onto a city street and not know where that danger lurked. Everyone looked suspicious: from the cab driver waiting at the traffic lights, to the elderly woman pulling a shopping cart at Gristede's, to the familiar doorman who tipped his hat each time Flynn and Jack walked past.

The day after their confrontation, O'Neal had come back and brought his wife along with him. Joanna was also part of the organization called PAX, and Flynn had found herself oddly comforted by the calm professionalism of the beautiful makeup wizard.

"Do you have any idea how O'Neal plans on protecting you?" she asked Jack on the fourth day as they waited for the elevator in his apartment building.

"He outlined a couple of ideas."

"Such as?"

He looked vaguely uncomfortable and that didn't add to Flynn's sense of well-being. "Nothing worth talking about. The guy's got one hell of an imagination."

The elevator doors slid open and they stepped inside. Just as the doors started to slide closed, a delivery boy with a huge basket of flowers slipped in with them. Flynn's heart beat double-time and she inched closer to Jack, whose back was pressed against the rear of the car.

"Hot outside, ain't it?" The delivery boy's smile was wide and cheerful.

Flynn nodded. Jack managed an unfriendly grunt.

The delivery boy peered at Flanagan over the basket of butter-yellow mums and lemon freesia. "You who I think you are?"

Jack shrugged and said nothing. Flynn prayed she wouldn't hyperventilate.

"You are," said the delivery boy. "You're Wild Man Flanagan."

"Yeah, well, keep it to yourself, okay?"

The delivery boy moved closer. "You were great in that fight. Cousin of mine got a friend who bought a black market tape of the Curtis fight. Best thing he ever saw."

Flanagan nodded. "Lenny Curtis is a great fighter."

The delivery boy was close enough for Flynn to smell the pollen. "You gonna fight again?"

Jack shook his head.

"Sure you are," said the delivery boy. "Big young guy like you. You're too young to retire."

"Please!" Flynn couldn't help herself. "We were in the middle of a private conversation."

The delivery boy narrowed his eyes. He put the basket of flowers down on the floor of the elevator and reached into his breast pocket.

Unfortunately that was all he had time to do before Jack had him pinned against the door and gasping for breath.

"Jack!" Flynn screamed.

"Frisk him," Jack ordered.

The delivery boy didn't know whether to be worried or delighted. She patted the boy's arms and legs and did a cursory check of the torso.

"Clean," she said.

"I could've told you that," the delivery boy grumbled as he tucked his shirt back into his cutoffs. "No wonder they call you Wild Man."

Jack didn't crack a smile. Flynn felt terrible and slipped the kid five dollars. The last thing they needed was more publicity.

Flynn snooped around Jack's apartment while he gathered up some of his things. O'Neal suggested Flanagan move into Flynn's apartment since her building was easier to secure, and neither Flynn nor Jack had taken exception. It was hard for her to imagine spending an extra second away from Flanagan—especially now that danger looked them squarely in the face.

Before they left Jack placed a call to Oscar in Boston. "Don't worry about anything," he told his trainer. "I won't forget the press conference next week...no, you stay put...I'll be fine...I'll tell her." He laughed and Flynn blushed. "In fact, you can reach me at Flynn's apartment from tonight on."

"How is he?" Flynn asked as they left the apartment.

"He's happy," Jack said.

"And healthy?"

Jack nodded. "Raising hell in the hospital. His sister says the nurses are threatening to boycott his room." He grinned. "But mostly he's happy."

"About us?"

"About us."

"I'm glad," said Flynn. "He had his reservations, you know."

Jack shrugged and took her hand. "Like I said, he's been a father to me. Can't blame him for wanting the best for his son." He laughed at the look of uncertainty she knew flickered across her face. "You've passed muster, Flynn. He wants us to name our first-born after him."

The walk home was uneventful, but Flynn found herself watching each passerby, every taxicab and bus, and wondering when the ax would fall.

They stayed in that night and the next day. It was almost possible to believe the outside world didn't exist, that O'Neal and his warnings had been part of a particularly bad dream.

Within the four walls of her apartment they created their own world, a world of intense emotional and sensual exploration. There was pleasure to be found in making love with Flanagan, but to Flynn's surprise, there was strength to be found in his arms, as well.

Another two days passed. Both Flynn and Jack tried to maintain a semblance of normalcy, but it proved more difficult with each hour.

On the sixth morning after the O'Neals' visit, Flynn had an assignment up at the Cloisters. Quiet, secluded, thick with lilac bushes where Marjorie Morningstar walked in the rain. They dressed her in a diaphanous gown of white lawn trimmed in hand-made lace. They posed her in front of the Unicorn tapestry—the perfect maiden.

They couldn't believe it when she dropped to the floor and covered her head with her hands.

"Flynn baby, you've been living in Manhattan too long," said the photographer. "That was only a flashgun, not an AK-47."

It was an hour before she stopped trembling long enough to have her picture taken.

JACK WASN'T FARING much better. The next afternoon he stepped out to hunt up the latest issue of *Sports Illustrated* and ended up crouching in the doorway of a Chinese restaurant.

"You need a vacation, Wild Man," said a passerby. "That was only a truck backfiring."

It took him the rest of the afternoon to bring his heart rate back down to anything approaching normal.

He couldn't help thinking about O'Neal. The guy was so sure that Jack was the only one in danger, that no harm would come to Flynn, that he almost had Jack convinced.

Almost but not quite.

Hell, he'd been like O'Neal once himself, so busy watching for the left jab that he never saw the right hook coming. High-tech gadgets and fancy security systems were no substitute for keeping your eyes open.

He intended to watch out for that right hook.

ON THE TENTH MORNING after the O'Neals' visit, Flynn polished her two thousand word piece on the fight and walked it over to the offices of *Sports Weekly*. She laughed with Stanley Moses and the gang and bore up under their relentless teasing with remarkable good grace.

Walking home, a construction worker whistled at her, and she found herself smiling back at him.

Jack had still been asleep when she left. Maybe she would pop into Bagel Stop and get the fixings for a real New York breakfast.

"Four onion with cream cheese," she said to the counter clerk. "A container of orange juice and two coffees to go." The clerk nodded and got to work.

Flynn looked out the huge storefront window while she waited. The usual midweek chaos reigned. Messengers dodging the traffic on ten-speed bikes. Businessmen and -women running to their appointments. Cabs and buses jockeying for position on the clogged streets. Nothing stopped New York. Not heat waves or crime waves or—

She spotted a slender man at the corner. He wore a pale beige summer suit. His hair was perfectly barbered with a European attention to detail. He raised his hand to hail a cab.

"Thomas." She stepped outside the shop. "Thomas!" she called out, but a cab screeched to a halt at the corner and the man climbed in.

She called Ryder O'Neal when she got back to the apartment. "I know it was my uncle's assistant," she said as Jack unpacked the take-out breakfast on the kitchen counter. "The question is, what's he doing in

New York?'' With the approaching Summit Conference, Judd's place would be with her uncle in Geneva.

She motioned for Jack to pick up the extension in the hallway.

"This is the sign we've been waiting for," said O'Neal.

"The press conference tomorrow?" asked Jack.

"The press conference tomorrow," said O'Neal.

In less than twenty-four hours she'd know whether their story would end happily-ever-after.

O'NEAL CAME BY LATER to review their plan. Flynn dug up some photos of Thomas Judd with her uncle. "I've seen that guy," said Jack, studying one of the pictures. "I've seen him around the neighborhood this week."

Flynn found it difficult to keep her emotions under control. Control was everything. The element of surprise was on the side of her uncle's henchmen but, thanks to Ryder and Joanna, they now had a few surprises of their own tucked up their sleeves.

She prayed it would be enough.

Neither Flynn nor Jack had much appetite for dinner. A little after ten o'clock they turned out the lights and lay together atop her four-poster bed, listening to the city traffic beneath her window.

He took her hand and held it to his chest. She felt the steady beating of his heart against her fingertips, and after a while her breathing slowed to match his. Such a small thing, to be attuned to another human being, but it seemed to Flynn as if the stars had gathered right there in her bedroom for Jack and for her.

She curled on her side, her breasts brushing lightly against the powerful muscle of his upper arm. She heard the low intake of breath, felt the sudden acceleration of his pulse, and desire—hot and urgent—rose up between them like a third presence in the darkened room.

For years she had moved in a world where illusion was everything. Beauty and wit passed for goodness and humanity, and few people, if any, ever questioned the difference.

With Flanagan it was different. He was as strong and courageous as he looked, as beautiful within as he was without. A real man in an era of imitations. He deserved so much better than this.

He kissed her eyelids, the tip of her nose, her chin.

She wished she could stop time and live in that moment forever. But she couldn't. The clock was ticking for both of them, and she had to make him understand before it was too late.

"This never should have happened," she said, cradling his face in her hands. "We've been walking around these past few weeks as if this was a normal case of boy-meets-girl." He started to say something, but she touched his lips with her index finger. "Extraordinary forces have been at work, Flanagan, forces we'll never be able to understand." Their first meeting had been at death's door. Their second meeting opened the gates of heaven. "Do you know how it feels to have another chance at happiness?"

He didn't answer but neither did he do anything to hide the play of emotions that flickered over his face. The mythical warrior tamed by the love of a woman. It was the greatest gift he could have given to her.

"All my life I've let other people take care of me, Jack. Now you're back in my life, and I've been willing to lean on you and let you bear the burden the same way I let all those other men care for me."

"I want to care for you, Flynn. That's the way it should be."

"No!" Her vehemence surprised them both. "That's not the way it should be. You pulled me out of the burning limo, Jack, but *I'm* the one who decided to live." She softened her tone and prayed he would understand what was ultimately beyond explanation. "I can do it, Jack. I can love you the way you deserve to be loved. I can step out of myself and give you what you need, but there may not be time, and that's the one thing I can't abide."

He pulled her close. "Nothing's going to happen to me, Flynn. Two weeks from now we'll be past all of this, and then we can talk about marriage and babies and the rest of our lives."

She moved away from him and met his eyes. "That's what Billy said." The words lingered in the air.

"It's all ahead of us, Flynn," he said, drawing her into his embrace. "I promise you. As soon as this is over, I'll make sure all of your dreams come true."

Please, God, she thought as she surrendered herself to his kiss. *Please give us the gift of time....*

He felt the subtle change in her touch instantly. The curve of her body grew more inviting, her skin felt more velvety and soft beneath his lips as he moved his way across her collarbone to the welcoming roundness of her breasts. The need to erase the boundaries between them, to forget where he ended and she began, was as ancient and powerful as the need for food and shelter.

That night in Flynn's arms, Jack finally discovered what he would do with the rest of his life. He'd toyed with real estate and considered movies and even played with the idea of maybe fighting just one more fight. But it took loving Flynn to make him understand that what he wanted most of all was to live. *Really* live. He wanted to marry her. To have children with her. To step back long enough to appreciate the miracle that had transformed his life into something more wonderful than the dreams he'd dreamed as a kid on the streets of Brooklyn.

This was the reason he'd struggled for so long to make a place for himself in the world. For Flynn. For her respect. Her love.

He moved his hand gently across her hip then brought it to rest against the inward curve of her belly. Her skin was smooth and cool to his touch, velvet against his open palm. He wondered how she would look swollen with his child. He'd never thought about children before, about sharing that ultimate connection with the woman he loved but lying there next to Flynn, he felt the need to see the love they shared sent forward into the next century and beyond.

They were forever. What they had would last. He couldn't believe fate had brought them back together only to have the last laugh.

It had been years since he'd asked God for anything, years since he'd believed in anyone but himself, but he found himself offering up a simple prayer that no matter what might happen tomorrow, the woman he loved would be spared.

THE HOTEL BALLROOM was noisy, smoky and packed full. From her vantage point near the side door the next morning, Flynn recognized a number of the reporters there from the title fight in the Bahamas. It seemed like another lifetime.

Flanagan was swept up to the dais by Ryder O'Neal and Joanna, who were posing as hotshot publicists. Joanna's makeup techniques were amazing; Flynn could have passed either one on the street and not recognized them.

Heart thudding, Flynn slipped into the end seat nearest the door.

Everything looked so average, so run-of-the-mill, that Flynn was having trouble believing that danger could hide behind such ordinary surroundings. For a moment she thought she saw Thomas Judd sitting in the back row, but then she looked again, he was gone. Imagination, she thought. Her nerves were taking over.

"Greetings, ladies and gentlemen," said a dark-haired man in a beige suit. "We're about to begin our around-the-world press conference with..."

The words tumbled around inside Flynn's brain. Flanagan looked so alone up there, so vulnerable. O'Neal had shown up at her apartment to escort them to the hotel for the conference. He had handed Jack a package, then sent him into the bedroom to change into the custom-tailored suit Ryder had brought with him. "Forget it," Jack had said. "I don't need your clothes."

"If you want to wake up tomorrow morning you do," said O'Neal. "These clothes are made of Kevlar."

She sat there, her head swimming with facts and figures. O'Neal had guaranteed the special clothing. He had detailed the strength of the fibers and hailed the remarkable technology that had made such a wonderful thing possible. A bullet to the chest would never find its target. She caught Jack's eye, and her own chest constricted at the smile he gave her.

And then it happened.

The sharp crack of gunshot echoed throughout the room.

"Get down!" screamed the man next to her. "Some lunatic's shot the champ!"

This is it...this is it...Ryder will take care of everything...Jack is safe...a bullet can't get through that suit...in another minute or two this will be over...

"Are you crazy?" The man next to her grabbed her arms and pulled her to the floor. "That lunatic is still shooting!"

Adrenaline was a miraculous thing. She overpowered the two hundred pounder in the blink of an eye. O'Neal had promised a miracle and she had believed him. But still she had to see for herself.

It's an illusion, she told herself. *A trick of makeup and lighting... he's fine... he's fine...* Joanna had explained it all to her, and she understood that all things were possible. But dear God, the illusion was terrifying. The man she loved more than life was slumped forward on the dais, bleeding from a bullet wound to the chest.

Chaos reigned. O'Neal had a tall blond man in cuffs while Joanna held a gun on him. Men she recognized as part of O'Neal's entourage struggled to control the crowd and guard the doors while they waited for the police to show up.

Until her dying day she would never know exactly why she did it, but Flynn tore her eyes away from Jack and turned just in time to see Thomas Judd slip out the side door and disappear down the hallway.

She hesitated a fraction of a second then slipped out the door after him.

Chapter Fourteen

Jack lay there on the ground counting slowly. One minute, O'Neal had said. Sixty seconds after the last gunshot and Jack could stand up—a miracle!—and the whole damn thing would be a memory.

Everything was going according to schedule except for one thing. Flynn should have been at his side by now.

He opened one eye a crack. O'Neal was busy cuffing some blond guy while Joanna kept a gun aimed at his head. Strange. He was pretty sure he'd seen Thomas Judd lurking near the side door they'd entered from. He would've bet the farm Judd was working as his boss's trigger man.

No matter. From the looks of it O'Neal had things under control.

. . . fifty-eight . . . fifty-nine . . . sixty.

He stood up. A reporter from *Newsweek* screamed and fell to the floor in a dead faint. Later on Jack would find that funny. Right now all he wanted was to find Flynn.

Fake blood poured from the gel pack under his shirt. He probably looked like something from *Fri-*

day the 13th. He grabbed Joanna by the arm. "Where is she?" he screamed over the crowd.

"She was here a moment ago. I'll—"

He didn't let her finish her sentence. He wheeled around and headed for the side door.

There it was: the right hook in the guise of Thomas Judd.

And he hadn't seen it coming.

THINGS WEREN'T WORKING OUT quite the way Flynn had planned them.

She'd raced out the door after Judd, fueled by anger and adrenaline. Her only thought had been to delay her uncle's assistant until he could be apprehended.

Well, surprise. Judd was stronger and smarter than she'd figured.

He pushed her into a small office near the hotel kitchen and locked the door after them.

"Troublemaker." His face contorted with anger. "You should have been dead years ago."

A telephone rested on the credenza. She made a lunge for it but Judd was faster. He ripped the wires from the wall.

Flanagan, where are you? Where were Ryder O'Neal and his cohorts with their twenty-first century weapons?

Judd withdrew a line of nylon cord from his pocket and pulled it taut between his hands. "You know, your uncle's a fool. You should've died along with your precious husband, but your uncle didn't think you'd cause any trouble."

That's it, Mary Flynn...don't worry your little head about it...you'll be rescued...someone will come for you....

Judd advanced. Her heart slammed against the wall of her chest. What if that shot had found its mark after all? What if Flanagan really was dead? What if O'Neal had been part of her uncle's plot?

What if the only person she could rely on was herself?

A scream tore her gut and lungs and throat.

"Scream all you want. With that commotion outside no one will ever hear you."

He grabbed for her, and in that instant her past fell away from her, and she was fighting for her future. She wanted to tear the flesh from his bones, dig her fingers into the bony sockets around his eyes, make him feel a fraction of the pain he'd caused her.

He turned her rage back on her. She hit the floor with a thud. Gasping for air, she fought to push him off but he had her pinned.

"Say good night, Mary Flynn." He began to wrap the nylon cord around her neck. "You're going to have a long, long sleep..."

In another second it would be all over. All her hopes and dreams gone forever. *Jack...I love you...I—*

Thomas Judd tightened the cord around her neck. She couldn't breathe, couldn't think, couldn't talk. She could, however, give him something to remember her by. Summoning up her last ounce of strength, she resorted to the only weapon she had left.

Judd's howl of pain rang out as her knee found its target.

The pressure on her windpipe stopped, and the room came back into focus just in time for her to see Flanagan break down the door.

Thomas Judd, still clutching where she'd kneed him, howled as if the very hounds of hell had him by the throat. "You're alive!"

"Looks that way, doesn't it?"

Flanagan, her beloved Flanagan, strode into the room as if he hadn't a care in the world. He was hale and hearty and blessedly, wondrously whole, and with one punch he knocked Thomas Judd out cold. She couldn't have done it better herself.

Flanagan crouched next to her on the ground, smoothing her hair, kissing the necklace of bruises that were blossoming on her pale skin. He murmured words of love she would hold close to her heart for the rest of her life.

"How did you know?" she asked, touching his cheek, his mouth, his forehead with trembling hands.

"I didn't." He kissed her and she tasted both fear and relief on his lips. "Not at first. I thought I'd imagined him in the audience, but when I stood up and saw you were missing, I knew."

He held her hand against the wild beating of his heart.

"You love me." Her words carried the weight of eternity.

"I love you," he said. "Marry me, Flynn. Let me spend the rest of our lives showing you exactly how much."

Her dark angel, her love.

Her husband.

"THEY'RE PERFECT for each other, aren't they?" Ryder O'Neal asked from the doorway after his men carried out an unconscious Thomas Judd.

"Just like us," said Joanna, squeezing his hand.

"You scared me when you walked out, Jo." He couldn't keep the emotion from his voice.

"Remember that the next time you decide to risk your life. I'm not just your wife; I'm your partner."

He nodded, not trusting his voice. It had been a long day. He'd been so single-minded in his pursuit of Hugh Scott that he had almost lost Mary Flynn along the way. How blind he'd been. How stupid. If it hadn't been for Flanagan—and the power of love—she would be dead.

For ten years Ryder had wanted to bring Hugh Scott to justice; today he had made the first important steps toward reaching that goal. He glanced at his watch. PAX was in motion; by midnight, New York time, Hugh Scott would be in custody.

Who would have imagined that not even that success could compare to what he felt for the woman at his side.

"I love you, Joanna," he said quietly, for her ears alone.

"Ah, Ryder," she said, taking his hand. "You always did have a way with words."

Two months later

THEY WERE ALL THERE, everyone who mattered, gathered in the garden of the O'Neals' Connecticut house. Jack's family had come from far and wide for the occasion. Friends Flynn had made along the way. Oscar, weak but feisty, on the arm of his sister.

And, of course, Ryder and Joanna. It wouldn't have been possible without them.

Father Dennehy, from the old church in Brooklyn, had come, too. He had baptized and married and buried three generations of Flanagans and had said wild horses couldn't keep him from performing the nuptials for Flynn and Jack.

When Jack saw her standing at the top of the path, he thought he'd died and an angel had come to fetch his soul. Her delicate, heart-shaped face was framed in ivory lace and he imagined the scent of violets in the air around him.

She made her way down the path toward where he stood by the oak tree. Her bearing was regal, the smile she gave him one of pure joy.

"You're beautiful," he said, as she slipped her arm in his. "My wife."

"Your wife," she said, moving into his strong arms. "For all time."

"Not until we stand before Father Dennehy."

"We've already stood before God, Flanagan. This is only a formality."

"Pretty important formality, wouldn't you say?"

"I'd say it was meant to be."

"Come on, Mary Flynn. It's time we got married."

And then beneath the spreading arms of the ancient oak, Mary Flynn Pennington and John James Flanagan did exactly that.

HARLEQUIN
American Romance®

COMING NEXT MONTH

HARLEQUIN
American Romance®
THE LOVES OF A CENTURY

Join American Romance in a nostalgic look back at the twentieth century—at the lives and loves of American men and women from the turn-of-the-century to the dawn of the year 2000.

Journey through the decades from the dance halls of the 1900's to the discos of the seventies...from Glenn Miller to the Beatles...from Valentino to Newman...from corset to miniskirt...from beau to significant other.

Relive the moments...recapture the memories.

Watch for all the CENTURY OF AMERICAN ROMANCE titles in Harlequin American Romance. In one of the four American Romance books appearing each month, for the next nine months, we'll take you back to a decade of the twentieth century, where you'll relive the years and rekindle the romance of days gone by.

Don't miss a day of A CENTURY OF AMERICAN ROMANCE.

A CENTURY OF
AMERICAN ROMANCE
1920ˢ

The women...the men...the passions...the memories...

Harlequin Intrigue.

REBECCA YORK

Labeled a "true master of intrigue" by *Rave Reviews*, best-selling author Rebecca York makes her Harlequin Intrigue debut with an exciting suspenseful new series.

It looks like a charming old building near the renovated Baltimore waterfront, but inside 43 Light Street lurks danger . . . and romance.

Let Rebecca York introduce you to:

> *Abby Franklin*—a psychologist who risks everything to save a tough adventurer determined to find the truth about his sister's death. . . .
> *Jo O'Malley*—a private detective who finds herself matching wits with a serial killer who makes her his next target. . . .
> *Laura Roswell*—a lawyer whose inherited share in a development deal lands her in the middle of a murder. And she's the chief suspect. . . .

These are just a few of the occupants of 43 Light Street you'll meet in Harlequin Intrigue's new ongoing series. Don't miss any of the 43 LIGHT STREET books, beginning with #143 LIFE LINE.

And watch for future LIGHT STREET titles, including #155 SHATTERED VOWS (February 1991) and #167 WHISPERS IN THE NIGHT (August 1991).

HI-143-1

Harlequin Superromance ®

THE LIVING WEST

Where men and women must be strong in both body
and spirit; where the lessons of the past must be fully
absorbed before the present can be understood; where
the dramas of everyday lives are played out against a
panoramic setting of sun, red earth, mountain and
endless sky....

Harlequin Superromance is proud to present this
powerful new trilogy by Suzanne Ellison, a veteran
Superromance writer who has long possessed a
passion for the West. Meet Joe Henderson, whose past
haunts him—and his romance with Mandy Larkin;
Tess Hamilton, who isn't sure she can make a life with
modern-day pioneer Brady Trent, though she loves
him desperately; and Clay Gann, who thinks the
cultured Roberta Wheeler isn't quite woman enough
to make it in the rugged West....

Please join us for HEART OF THE WEST (September
1990), SOUL OF THE WEST (October 1990) and
SPIRIT OF THE WEST (November 1990) and see the
West come alive!

SR-LW-420-1